When The Bell Rings

Fidel Monte

BMN Publishing

Contents

Prologue

Mateo Aragon had always been a quiet soul, an observer of life's ebb and flow within the sleepy town of San Agustin. Nestled between rolling hills and meandering rivers, the town seemed suspended in time, untouched by the chaos of the outside world. Every cobblestone street held stories of generations past, and every weathered building whispered secrets carried on the winds of history.

Mateo's heart had been sensitive to the whispers of the world around him since his early years. He found solace in the ancient chapel that stood at the heart of San Agustin, its time-worn walls bearing witness to countless prayers and quiet contempla- tion. As he sat in the pew, watching the soft light filter through stained glass windows, he felt a pull, an invisible thread connecting him to something larger than himself.

His family, like many in the town, held steadfast to their traditions, their lives intricately woven into the fabric of San Agustin's past. Yet, as the years rolled on, Mateo's heart carried a burden that set him apart. While his friends dreamed of worldly pursuits, he found himself drawn to the tales of saints and martyrs, their unwavering faith igniting a fire within him.

It was on a summer evening, the sky painted with hues of orange and gold, that Mateo's path began to reveal itself. He stood by the riverbank, the water's gentle rhythm mirroring the thoughts that swirled within him. His parents, both hardworking and humble, had sacrificed so much to ensure his future. But as the sun dipped beneath the horizon, a calling beckoned him, a whisper carried by the breeze that spoke of a life devoted to service.

Mateo spent his nights in fervent prayer in the following weeks, seeking guidance and clarity. One Sunday morning, right after the mass, Mateo approached Father Gabriel, the parish priest of San Agustin, and asked for some advice about his decision to enter the seminary in the coming school year opening. Fr. Gabriel recognized the flame that burned within Mateo's soul. Their conversations were filled with discussions about faith, sacrifice, and the profound responsibility that came with serving God's people. Mateo hung onto every word, the weight of his calling settling upon his shoulders with a mix of awe and trepidation.

As the day of his high school graduation approached, a choice loomed before him like a crossroads. The path he was about to tread was not one of glamour or fame, but of quiet devotion and steadfast loyalty. Yet, even as he considered the sacrifices, there was a certainty that anchored him. It was as if the very stones of San Agustin whispered to him, echoing the footsteps of ancestors who had chosen similar paths.

On the day of his graduation, as the community gathered to celebrate its young minds, Mateo stood at the podium with a heart full of gratitude. His eyes scanned the faces of those who had shaped his journey: his parents, his friends, and the priest who had become a guiding light. And in that moment, as he spoke of dreams and futures, there was a subtle undercurrent, a thread that tied his words to something deeper, something that held the key to the true reason behind his calling.

As the ceremony concluded, Mateo walked through the streets of San Agustin, the town's history unfolding beneath his feet. He passed the chapel, its bells tolling the hour with a melody that seemed to resonate with the cadence of his heartbeat. It was here, in this place of quiet reverence, that he finally allowed his mind to touch the edges of the truth.

The true reason behind his calling was a secret buried deep within the cobblestones of San Agustin, a tale that intertwined his journey with the town's own. It was a story of pain and resilience, of love and sacrifice, a story that had woven its way into the very fabric of his being. And as he gazed at the chapel's ancient walls, Mateo felt a profound connection, a knowing that his path was not just his own but a continuation of a legacy that had begun long before him.

Unbeknownst to Mateo, as the chapel's bells tolled that evening, they carried with them the echoes of generations, a chorus of souls who had walked similar paths of devotion and self-discovery. And as the sun dipped below the horizon, casting a warm glow over the town, Mateo felt a sense of peace settle within him. The calling that had beckoned him was not just a whisper in the wind; it was a symphony of voices that had shaped his destiny, a destiny intricately woven into the tapestry of San Agustin's history.

CHAPTER I

The Bell's Melody

From the moment Mateo stepped through the arched gates of the diocesan seminary, he felt a change in the air, a weighty stillness that seemed to press gently on his shoulders. The seminary grounds, tucked away in a quiet corner of the diocese, were surrounded by towering oaks and pines, their shadows stretching across the worn stone paths like fingers. A weathered crucifix stood at the center of the courtyard, arms outstretched as though embracing all who sought refuge there. And there was the bell—a brass sentinel high in the tower—silent for now, but ready to mark each passage of the day.

That first morning, as the sun barely peeked over the tree line, Mateo lay awake in his narrow bed, listening. The dormitory was filled with the quiet breaths of other young men who, like him, had chosen a path of service. His heart beat quickly with a mix of anticipation and uncertainty. He wondered if any of the others could sense it too—the strange feeling of being on the cusp of something profound and unyielding.

Then, it rang.

The bell's chime was slow and deliberate, cutting through the early morning hush like a pebble tossed into still waters. Mateo felt it resonate within him, a sound that seemed to connect heaven and earth. He sat up quickly, the sound vibrating in his chest as he pulled on his simple black robe and joined the line of sleepy seminarians heading for morning prayers. No words were exchanged, only the quiet shuffle of feet on cold stone floors.

In those early days, the bell seemed to be everywhere, its presence weaving through the fabric of Mateo's life like a golden thread. It was there at dawn, nudging him awake before the sun could rise fully. It was there in the late afternoon when shadows stretched long and thin across the seminary courtyard, calling him to evening vespers. It was there at night, in the silence that followed the last prayer, when Mateo lay awake in his bunk, feeling the lingering echoes reverberate through his thoughts.

He began to recognize the bell not merely as an instrument of timekeeping but as a presence, something that guided and shaped their lives. Each time it tolled, he found himself wondering what it wanted of him, what it sought to teach. The older seminarians moved with a practiced ease, seeming to anticipate the bell's next call, but Mateo still felt like he was catching up—an outsider trying to attune himself to this new, unyielding rhythm.

In the chapel, under the soft glow of candlelight, the prayers began—whispered Latin phrases that Mateo had studied and memorized in the weeks before arriving. As the words rolled off his tongue, he felt a strange comfort in their familiarity, even though he was still learning to grasp their full meaning. The chapel smelled of incense and polished wood, a scent that reminded him of San Agustin's own modest church. But here, in this grand space where stained-glass saints watched over them, everything felt larger, more intense.

And always, as he knelt and spoke the ancient words, San Agustin lingered at the edges of his mind like a shadow. It crept in during the pauses between prayers, slipping into his thoughts like a visitor. He would recall the church in his hometown—humble but warm, filled with the earthy scent of wooden pews worn smooth by generations. He would remember the people who filled those pews, their faces furrowed with struggles and joys, and the way they looked to Father Gabriel for comfort and guidance. He wondered what they would think of him now, walking among these high stone walls, chasing the echoes of the bell.

After morning prayers came breakfast, and Mateo discovered that life in the seminary was as much about the simple rhythms of daily existence as it was about divine calling. Meals were shared at long wooden tables, with silence broken only by the occasional laughter or the murmur of a verse. The food was plain—thick porridge, bread that was sometimes a little stale—but it filled them, just as the Scriptures they read filled their hearts. The bell rang again, summoning them to their first class.

Each lesson was a step deeper into the mysteries of faith. The subjects of theology, philosophy, and church history required both a sharp mind and a willing spirit. Father Alvarez, an older priest with kind but unyielding eyes, led the classes. He had served as the seminary's academic guide for decades, his voice worn with years of sermons and confessions. He would pace before the blackboard, spinning stories of the ancient Church fathers, their struggles, and their unwavering devotion. Mateo took notes diligently, but there was an unease within him—an itch that the knowledge alone could not scratch.

He listened to the stories of Saint Augustine and Saint Francis, men who had given up their worldly attachments for a life of piety. Yet he couldn't ignore the thought that gnawed at him: what was *his* reason for being here? The question was like a splinter under his skin, something he couldn't quite reach but that made its presence known in moments of quiet.

The bell rang to signal midday, drawing them back to the chapel for the Angelus prayer. And later, it rang again for lunch, then study time, then manual labor. Mateo often found himself assigned to the gardens, where he pulled weeds from the flowerbeds that framed the seminary grounds. He found a certain peace in the repetitive task, the scent of soil mingling with the distant hum of insects. Yet, there was always that subtle pressure in the back of his mind, a shadow that grew larger as he labored in the sun. He couldn't help but wonder why he alone seemed to feel its weight.

It was during these solitary moments in the garden, kneeling among the rows of chrysanthemums and lavender, that he felt closest to the memories of San Agustin. He could see the river that wound its way past the edge of town and the way the light shimmered on its surface during summer evenings.

He could hear the murmur of voices in the town square, the laughter of children, and the clinking of cups at the café where the old men sat and talked of days long gone. And occasionally, he thought of the faces—faces that had grown sadder over time, as if they, too, carried secrets they could not speak aloud.

One evening, as the bell announced vespers and the sky outside burned with the deep hues of sunset, Mateo lingered in the chapel after the others had left. The air was cool and fragrant with incense, the only light coming from the flickering candles beneath the Virgin Mary's statue. He knelt, pressing his hands together, and tried to empty his mind, to let the prayers flow through him. But images from San Agustin pushed their way into his thoughts—memories of the riverbank, of his mother's weary smile, of late-night conversations with Father Gabriel where words were exchanged in hushed tones.

What was it about those memories that stirred him so deeply? Mateo couldn't yet articulate it, but it was there, a thread that tied his words to something deeper, something that held the key to the true reason behind his calling.

The chapel, of course, offered no reply. But the weight of that question settled over him like a shroud, mingling with the incense that curled toward the ceiling. Mateo let out a slow breath and rose to his feet, stepping out into the night air. The seminary grounds were dark, with only the distant glow of the dormitory windows to guide him. He looked up at the bell tower, the ancient structure silhouetted against a canopy of stars, and wondered how long it would be before he understood the fullness of his calling.

As he turned toward the dormitory, Mateo realized that his days would continue to be dictated by the bell's steady rhythm—rising, falling, like breaths of a life that was both new and ancient. He knew that the truth behind his calling would not reveal itself all at once. It would come slowly, slipping through the cracks of routine and the spaces between each toll of the bell.

For now, all he could do was follow its rhythm, trusting that somewhere within its ringing lay the answers to the questions that stirred in his heart. And perhaps, in time, the bell would guide him not only through the routines of the seminary but also toward the hidden parts of himself that had been shaped by San Agustin—those quiet shadows that would, eventually, demand to be faced.

Chapter 2

Unveiling the Silence

Days at the seminary settled into a predictable rhythm, each hour outlined with precision, and every action choreographed by the tolling of the bell. But despite the seeming monotony, each day held its own challenges, its own subtle shifts in the fabric of time. Mateo soon realized that life here was like living inside a clock, where every gear and cog moved with purpose, yet hidden beneath that mechanical regularity was a place where the mind could wander and the spirit could struggle.

It was during these early days that Mateo began to see his fellow seminarians with clearer eyes. There was Emilio, a tall, wiry boy from a coastal town whose sunburned cheeks and quick smile made him a favorite among the group. He approached the studies with a fervor that bordered on zeal, often staying up late with a small oil lamp, tracing the fine script of Latin in his worn notebook. Emilio spoke often of his family's fishing business and the sacrifices they made so he could study here, but in the quiet moments, Mateo could see a restlessness in his gaze, as if the sea still called to him.

Then there was Tomás, a heavyset young man with a somber face and a voice that rumbled like distant thunder. He was the eldest of the seminarians and had already spent several years in the seminary, yet he seemed to bear the weight of the world on his shoulders. His prayers were deep and fervent, his voice filling the chapel with a resonance that seemed to touch the stones themselves. Mateo often noticed Tomás standing alone at the edge of the courtyard, his hands clasped behind his back as he stared at the bell tower, lost in thoughts that he never shared with the others.

Mateo felt a kinship with these young men, yet a distance as well, a gap that he could not fully close. Emilio's easy jokes often made him smile, and Tomás' deep faith was something to aspire to, yet Mateo sensed that his own reasons for being here were different, perhaps even murkier. It was not something he could put into words, even to himself, but it lingered like a shadow, slipping into his mind during the quiet spaces between the bell's calls.

The seminary's daily routines left little room for introspection, but it was in those moments when the bell's voice was silent that Mateo felt the old memories creeping in. One evening, after the bell had announced the end of evening prayers and the sky turned a deep indigo, he found himself sitting alone on the edge of the courtyard, watching the stars emerge from the darkening sky. The air was cool, and the distant chirping of crickets filled the spaces that the bell had left behind.

As Mateo traced the constellation of Orion with his eyes, he thought of nights in San Agustin when he would sit by the riverbank, listening to the water's soft murmur and wondering what lay beyond the hills that surrounded his small town. In those moments, he had dreamed of a different life—a life where he might find purpose, where he could become someone who made a difference. But alongside those dreams were memories he did not want to confront, memories that made his chest tighten and his thoughts turn inward.

He could still see his mother's face, lined with worry, as she stood at their front door, bidding him farewell when he left for the seminary. Her smile had been forced, her eyes glassy with tears she tried to hide. Mateo wondered if she had sensed the weight he carried, the unspoken reasons that had driven him to leave their home behind. He had assured her that he wanted to serve God, that he was called to a life of faith, but he could never quite escape the feeling that she had seen through the cracks in his words.

With a sigh, Mateo leaned back, resting his head against the rough stone of the seminary wall. He closed his eyes, letting the cool night air brush over his face. A part of him wished he could speak openly about what lay buried within him, but the words remained lodged in his throat, tangled and uncertain. He thought of Father Gabriel's last words to him before he left San Agustin: *"The Lord knows your heart, even when you cannot find the words. Trust in that, Mateo."*

But trusting was easier said than done.

A rustle of footsteps on the path pulled Mateo from his thoughts. He turned to see Tomás approaching, his broad silhouette outlined against the fading light. Tomás paused a few steps away, his hands still clasped behind his back as he gazed at the sky.

"You seem troubled, hermano," Tomás said quietly, his voice carrying a gravity that Mateo had come to recognize. "The night has a way of bringing our thoughts to the surface, doesn't it?"

Mateo hesitated, unsure how much to reveal. "It does, Tomás. Sometimes I find myself thinking a bout... everything. About why I'm here, what I'm meant to become. Do you ever feel that way?"

Tomás turned to look at him, his expression thoughtful. "Every day. But I've learned that those questions don't always have answers, not right away. The bell teaches us patience, you know. It rings when it's time to pray, to work, to reflect. But it never rushes. Perhaps we must learn to wait as it does."

They sat together in silence for a while, the darkness deepening around them, punctuated only by the faint glow of the seminary windows. Mateo found a strange comfort in Tomás' presence, a sense that he was not entirely alone in his struggles. Yet he also sensed that Tomás, too, carried his own burdens, unspoken but heavy.

The next morning, the bell rang early, pulling them all from their dreams. Mateo rose, slipping into his robe and joining the procession to the chapel. The rhythm of life continued, each hour carved out by the bell's clear tones, but Mateo felt a subtle shift within himself. The questions that had haunted him remained, but he began to see that perhaps the answers would come not in a flash of revelation, but in the slow unfolding of time.

Classes with Father Alvarez became more intense, the subjects digging deeper into the complexities of faith. They debated the nature of grace, the writings of Augustine and Aquinas, and the tension between free will and divine providence. Sometimes, Mateo's mind wandered to San Agustin during these discussions—particularly to moments when Father Gabriel spoke of suffering and redemption, of finding God in the darkest corners of life. Mateo wondered if his decision to enter the seminary was his way of searching for that light, or if he was still trying to outrun a shadow that followed him from the town he'd left behind.

During one lecture, Father Alvarez paused, his gaze sweeping over the class. "A true vocation is not merely the desire to serve," he said, his voice low but steady. "It is a willingness to confront the self, to stand naked before God and face the parts of us that we would rather hide. It is not an escape, but a journey inward, toward the deepest parts of the soul."

The words struck Mateo like a bell tolling in his mind, reverberating through the thoughts he had kept buried. *A journey inward.* He repeated the phrase to himself, feeling its weight. The bell called them to prayer then, and as Mateo knelt in the chapel, he let the silence fill him, hoping it might reveal something he had not yet found the courage to see.

As the days passed, Mateo continued to listen for the answers within that silence, even as the bell rang on, guiding him through the routines of seminary life. He followed its rhythm with the rest, but in the quiet spaces between each chime, he felt something shifting within him, a slow peeling back of layers he had long kept hidden. And though he still could not articulate what lay at the heart of his calling, he sensed that the bell's melody was drawing him closer to the truth, one slow, deliberate toll at a time.

CHAPTER 3

Beneath the Surface

The days at the seminary continued to unfold with a regularity that could almost be mistaken for peace. Mateo followed the bell's call, moving from prayer to study, from meals to labor, and from morning to night. Yet as the weeks passed, he realized that the seminary, with all its rules and rituals, did not quiet the questions inside him. Rather, it amplified them, as if each toll of the bell resonated with an unanswered question in his heart.

The crisp autumn air began to settle over the seminary grounds, bringing with it a quiet chill that seeped into the ancient stone walls. Mateo found himself drawn to the gardens more often during their free hours, preferring the solitude among the dying leaves and withering flowers. The other seminarians accepted his aloofness as part of his nature, but a few still sought to reach out, sensing a kindred spirit beneath his quiet demeanor.

It was during one of these afternoons in the garden that Mateo found himself working beside Emilio, whose effortless smile rarely faltered, even when faced with the stubborn roots of the garden's older shrubs. They labored side by side, pulling weeds and turning the soil in preparation for the winter frost. Emilio worked with the deft movements of someone used to physical labor, and for a while, they spoke only of trivial things—the changes in the weather, the next reading assignment in their theology class.

But eventually, as the sun dipped lower and cast long shadows across the garden beds, Emilio grew quieter. Mateo noticed the change, glancing sideways at his friend. There was a crease in Emilio's brow that he hadn't seen before, a shadow that matched the one in Mateo's own heart.

"Do you ever think about what comes after this?" Emilio asked suddenly, his voice low, almost lost beneath the rustling of the leaves. "Not just the ordination, but... the life beyond the seminary. The parish, the people. The weight of all that."

Mateo hesitated, considering the question. It was one he had asked himself many times in the quiet of the dormitory, late at night when sleep eluded him. "Sometimes," he admitted, keeping his voice just as soft. "I think about what it means to take on that responsibility. To be the one people look to for answers, for guidance. It feels... heavy."

Emilio let out a short, humorless laugh. "That's one word for it. Sometimes, I wonder if I'll be ready when the time comes. If any of us will be." He glanced at Mateo, a question in his eyes. "But you... you seem sure of yourself. Like you've known what you wanted for a long time."

Mateo felt the words catch in his throat. He opened his mouth, then closed it again, unsure of how to respond. In that moment, the truth hovered just out of reach, and he couldn't bring himself to grasp it. So he offered Emilio a tight smile instead, one that he hoped seemed reassuring.

"I think we all have our doubts," he said finally, turning back to the soil beneath his hands. But even as he spoke the words, he knew they rang hollow.

Later that evening, as they gathered in the chapel for vespers, Mateo found himself thinking about Emilio's question. He knelt among the rows of seminarians, their heads bowed in unison, but his thoughts were far from the psalms they chanted. He thought of San Agustin, of the winding river and the humble homes that clung to its banks. He thought of Father Gabriel's small parish, where hope and despair mingled in equal measure among the people who filled the pews on Sundays. He thought of his mother's hands, roughened from years of work, clasped together in prayer, asking for things Mateo had never dared to ask for himself.

The bell rang to close the evening prayer, pulling him from his reverie. The seminarians rose and moved in orderly lines back toward the dormitory, but Mateo lingered, feeling the echo of the bell's chime resonate in his bones. It was then that Father Alvarez, who often stayed behind to extinguish the candles and straighten the hymnals, caught sight of him.

"You have a troubled look about you, Mateo," the older priest remarked, his voice gentle but perceptive. "The chapel is a place for bringing our burdens to God, but you seem to carry yours back out with you."

Mateo hesitated, unsure how to respond. Father Alvarez's gaze was steady and patient, as if he could wait all night for an answer. Finally, Mateo spoke, choosing his words carefully. "It's just... sometimes I wonder if I'm truly meant to be here, Father. If my reasons for coming were... pure enough."

Father Alvarez's expression did not change, but there was a flicker of understanding in his eyes.

He walked over to a nearby pew and gestured for Mateo to sit beside him. "Purity of intention is a heavy mantle, Mateo," he said, his voice carrying the weariness of many years. "But God does not always call those who are certain. More often, He calls those who are willing to be shaped, even if that shaping is painful. It is not always easy to hear His voice clearly, but the important thing is that you listen."

Mateo felt the words settle into the depths of his mind, like seeds planted in uncertain soil. He wanted to believe them, to trust that his presence here was part of a greater plan. But the doubts lingered, like a fog that refused to lift. He thanked Father Alvarez quietly and made his way back to the dormitory, his steps slow and thoughtful.

That night, sleep eluded Mateo. He lay awake, listening to the rhythmic breathing of the others in the darkened room. He closed his eyes, trying to focus on the familiar sounds—the rustling of blankets, the occasional creak of the old wooden floors. But underneath it all, he could still hear the bell, faint and distant, like the heartbeat of the seminary itself.

And then, in the early hours of the morning, something happened that Mateo would carry with him for a long time. He awoke suddenly, not to the bell's call, but to a silence that was profound and total. For a moment, it felt as if the world had stopped spinning, as if he were suspended in a stillness so complete that it pressed against his ears.

In that silence, Mateo heard a different sound—one that he had not heard in years. It was the sound of water, the gentle flow of a river, carrying with it a whisper he could not quite decipher. He sat up in bed, straining to catch the fading echoes, but as quickly as it had come, the sound disappeared, leaving him alone in the darkness.

For the rest of the night, he lay awake, the memory of that fleeting moment stirring something deep within him. He could not shake the feeling that it meant something—that it was a message, a sign, though he did not yet understand what it was trying to tell him. When the bell finally rang for morning prayer, he rose from his bed with a strange sense of anticipation, as if he had glimpsed the edge of a mystery he was meant to unravel.

The following days passed as before, with the same routine and the same steady rhythm of work and study. But something had shifted within Mateo. He found himself listening more closely, not just to the bell that guided their days, but to the silences in between, to the pauses where meaning might dwell. He could not shake the image of the river, nor the sense that somehow, it was calling him back—back to a place, or a memory, or a truth he had yet to uncover.

And through it all, he carried the words of Father Alvarez with him, letting them echo in his mind like a prayer: *God calls those who are willing to be shaped.*

It was a comfort, but it was also a challenge, one that he knew he would need to confront. Mateo did not yet know where his journey would lead or what truths lay hidden within the recesses of his heart. But he understood one thing clearly: the bell was leading him somewhere, and whatever awaited him at the end of its steady tolling, he would face it with open hands and an uncertain heart.

CHAPTER 4

Mastering Delayed Gratification

Mateo had always been told that patience was a virtue, but it wasn't until he entered the seminary that he began to understand just how elusive that virtue could be. The seminary's life was a constant exercise in delayed gratification, where every small pleasure was measured against a backdrop of spiritual growth and discipline. The food was simple, the beds hard, and the comforts of home a distant memory. Yet, there was a purpose behind the austerity—one that Mateo tried to grasp, even as it eluded him like the last light of a setting sun.

The bell continued to dictate their lives, and with each chime, it reminded them that their time was not their own. The seminarians were expected to wait for everything: for meals, for rest, and for the rare moments when they could speak freely among themselves. This waiting was a lesson in itself, a way to strip away the distractions of the outside world and teach them to focus on what truly mattered. But for Mateo, the waiting brought something else as well: a kind of quiet frustration that he struggled to suppress.

It was during the long, unbroken hours of study that Mateo felt this frustration most acutely. Father Alvarez's lectures on the writings of Aquinas, Augustine, and the early Church fathers were rich and layered, but they often left Mateo feeling as though he was standing before a great mountain, unable to see the peak through the clouds. He admired the elegance of their arguments and the way they grappled with the nature of God and the mysteries of creation, but at times, he found himself yearning for answers that were more immediate and more tangible.

One afternoon, as the bell rang to signal the end of study and the beginning of manual labor, Mateo lingered in the library, surrounded by stacks of theological texts. The air was heavy with the smell of old paper and wood polish, the light streaming in through high windows dusted with autumn leaves. He turned a page in a worn volume of *Confessions* and read Augustine's words: *"You have made us for Yourself, O Lord, and our hearts are restless until they rest in You."*

The restlessness Augustine spoke of resonated deeply with Mateo. He felt that same restlessness within himself, a churning beneath the surface that all the rituals and prayers had not yet soothed. He wondered if Augustine, in all his wisdom, had ever felt as lost as he did now, struggling to reconcile the grand ideas of faith with the smallness of his own doubts.

Emilio appeared in the doorway then, a sheepish smile on his face as he gestured to the clock. "You're going to be late for the gardens, hermano. And you know how Father Domingo reacts when we fall behind.

Mateo closed the book reluctantly, slipping it back onto the shelf. He offered Emilio a small, grateful smile, but as he followed him out of the library, the uneasiness lingered, like a splinter that he couldn't quite dislodge. They walked together in silence, heading toward the gardens where Father Domingo, a strict but fair elder priest, awaited them.

The garden work that day involved harvesting the last of the autumn herbs before the frost set in. Mateo knelt among the rows of sage and rosemary, his hands moving mechanically as he pulled the fragrant sprigs from the earth. Yet his mind was elsewhere, still caught in the labyrinth of Augustine's words. He found himself envying the plants around him—their simple purpose, their quiet acceptance of the seasons. He wondered if he would ever find that same peace within himself, or if he would always be reaching, yearning, for something just out of his grasp.

As she worked, Mateo became aware of Tomás nearby, tending to a row of basil plants. The older seminarian moved with a calm, deliberate grace, his heavy hands surprisingly gentle as he gathered the herbs. Tomás caught Mateo's gaze and offered a knowing nod, as if sensing the turmoil within him.

"You know, Mateo," Tomás said after a long silence, his voice low and thoughtful, "sometimes I think we misunderstand what it means to wait. We think it's about enduring, about pushing through the discomfort until it's over. But perhaps it's more about learning to be present, even when the answers don't come."

Mateo paused, letting the words sink in. He looked down at the rosemary clutched in his hands, its scent rising sharply into the crisp air. "I know I should trust in the process, that I should be patient," he replied, his voice barely more than a whisper. "But sometimes I feel like I'm just... treading water. Waiting for something to happen, for some revelation to finally make sense of everything."

Tomás gave a small, understanding smile. "Revelation doesn't always come as a flash of light, hermano. Sometimes, it's more like the way a river carves its path through the rocks—slow, steady, almost imperceptible, until one day you look and see how much has changed."

Mateo nodded, not trusting himself to say more. But Tomás's words stayed with him long after they returned to their chores, and he took them into the chapel that evening as he knelt for prayer. As the bell rang out, calling them to vespers, he closed his eyes and tried to imagine himself as the river—slowly wearing away at the edges of his own uncertainty, trusting that one day, he might see the shape of what he was meant to become.

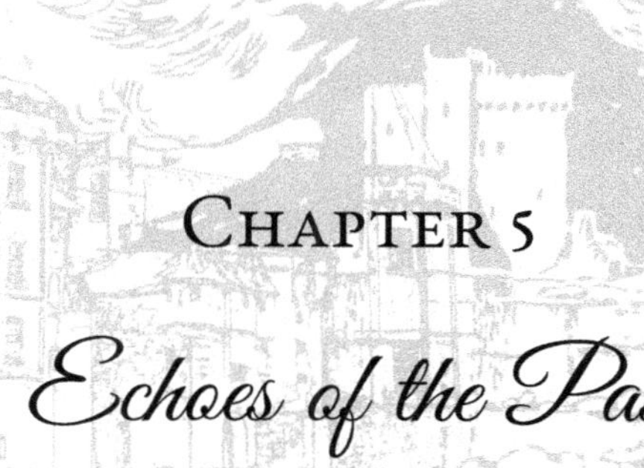

CHAPTER 5

Echoes of the Past

The first chill of winter settled over the seminary, and with it came a stillness that seemed to deepen the silence of the grounds. The trees, stripped of their leaves, stood like skeletal sentinels against the gray sky, and the wind carried the scent of distant snow. Inside the stone walls, the seminarians moved through routines as always, but the coming of winter seemed to bring a sharper edge to the air, a sense of something closing in.

For Mateo, the change in seasons brought a new wave of memories. The cold reminded him of winters in San Agustin—of the frost that crept up the windows of their small house and of his mother's hands wrapped in worn gloves as she lit the woodstove each morning. He remembered the way the river would slow and grow silent beneath a thin layer of ice, and how he would sometimes sit by the banks, watching his breath form clouds in the air.

One evening, as the seminarians gathered around the hearth in the common room, Mateo found himself drawn into conversation with Emilio and a few others. They spoke of their hometowns, sharing stories of childhood winters and the traditions that marked the season. Emilio regaled them with tales of the coastal storms that swept through his village, while another seminarian, Diego, described the elaborate Nativity scenes his family would build each year.

When it was Mateo's turn to share, he hesitated. He thought of San Agustin's simple Christmases, the modest decorations in the church, and the small gifts exchanged between neighbors. He thought of Father Gabriel's midnight Mass, where the church would fill with the sound of carols sung by voices roughened by cold air. But when he spoke, he found himself skirting around the edges of those memories, offering only the surface details.

"It was a quiet town," he said, staring into the flames as they crackled in the hearth. "We didn't have much, but there was always a sense of... togetherness. Like the whole town came together during the cold months, finding warmth in each other."

Emilio nodded thoughtfully, but Diego seemed to notice the hesitation in Mateo's voice. "You miss it, don't you?" he asked, his tone gentle but probing. "San Agustin. You speak of it like it's still a part of you."

Mateo swallowed, feeling the weight of the question. "I suppose I do," he admitted, his voice barely more than a murmur. "But sometimes it feels like... like it's a part of me that I can't quite reach anymore. Like something's been left behind."

The words seemed to hang in the air, heavy and unspoken. For a moment, Mateo considered sharing more details with them—specifically, the deeper reasons that had compelled him to leave San Agustin and the secrets he had carried across the riverbanks into the stone walls of the seminary. But the bell rang then, cutting through the conversation, and the moment slipped away like water through his fingers.

They rose from their seats and made their way to the chapel, but the questioning lingered in Mateo's mind as they knelt for prayer. He wondered if Diego had sensed something in his silence, or if the other seminarians felt the same unspoken distance between the life they had left behind and the life they were trying to build.

As he bowed his head, Mateo found himself praying not for answers but for the strength to carry the questions a little longer. He prayed for the patience that Tomás had spoken of, the kind that could endure the waiting without breaking. And in the silence that followed the bell's final toll, he thought he heard the faintest echo of a river—its voice buried beneath layers of time and memory, but still flowing, still carrying him toward something he could not yet see.

CHAPTER 6

Trials and Tribulations

Life at the seminary was never meant to be easy, but Mateo hadn't fully grasped how deeply it would test him until he faced his first real trials. In those early days, it seemed as though the challenges came at him from all sides—small things that gnawed at his patience, bigger struggles that chipped away at his sense of purpose. The bell rang, marking each new task, each call to prayer, and each moment of reflection, but for Mateo, the rhythm of those chimes had begun to feel less like a guide and more like a relentless pressure, bearing down on him day after day.

The first real test came during one of their scripture study sessions. Father Alvarez, with his stern but gentle manner, had assigned the seminarians a passage from the Book of Job, a meditation on suffering and divine will. They were to write a reflection, exploring the meaning of suffering and how it shapes a believer's relationship with God. For many, it was a chance to go beyond scripture with a sense of academic curiosity, to wrestle with the ancient text and determine its relevance to their lives. However, the assignment had a profound impact on Mateo.

As he read through the lines, he felt a quiet unease stir in him, a discomfort that lingered like the bite of the autumn air. Job's trials—the loss of his family, his health, his standing—were the sort of burdens that seemed almost abstract when discussed in the context of ancient times. But for Mateo, they felt like a mirror to his own unspoken struggles, a reflection of the silent burdens he carried from San Agustin.

He tried to write the reflection with the same analytical approach that his peers adopted, but the words refused to come. Instead, his mind wandered back to the faces of those he'd left behind, to the unspoken questions in his mother's eyes when he told her of his decision to join the seminary, and to the quiet conversations he had shared with Father Gabriel under the stars. The paper remained half-written, the thoughts fragmented and restless.

Father Alvarez noticed Mateo's distraction during the study sessions, and one afternoon, he called Mateo into his office. The room was small but cozy, its walls lined with shelves of theological books, and a cross hung prominently above the desk. As Mateo sat down, the old priest regarded him with a calm yet penetrating gaze, as if he could see straight through to the heart of the matter.

"Mateo," Father Alvarez began, folding his hands together. "I've noticed that you've been struggling with the scripture reflection. It's not uncommon, you know. The story of Job can be difficult to understand, even for those of us who have studied it for many years. But I sense that there's something more that's weighing on you."

Mateo looked down at his hands, which were clenched tightly in his lap. He felt exposed, as though the old priest had reached into the depths of his mind and pulled out all the tangled thoughts he had tried to hide. He took a deep breath, trying to gather his words, but what came out was halting and uncertain.

"I just... I don't know if I understand suffering, Father. I don't know if I understand why God allows it or how we're supposed to find meaning in it. When I think about Job, it makes me feel... small. Like I don't have the strength to endure what he did.

And sometimes, I wonder if I'm just running away from my own questions by being here."

Father Alvarez nodded slowly, his expression thoughtful. "The question of suffering is one of the greatest mysteries we face, Mateo. And it's true that none of us can fully understand God's will, not even those of us who have dedicated our lives to seeking it. But remember, Job did not endure his trials because he was without doubt. He endured them because he continued to wrestle with those doubts, to confront God even when he did not understand Him."

The words lingered with Mateo long after he left Father Alvarez's office. He returned to his dormitory that evening, staring at the half-written reflection on his desk, wondering what it meant to confront his doubts rather than bury them. He thought of the questions that had driven him to leave San Agustin—questions that he had never fully answered, even as he prayed and studied and immersed himself in the seminary's routines.

Yet no sooner had he begun to reflect on these deeper matters than another trial emerged—this time, one that tested his resolve in a far more tangible way.

It happened during one of their weekly chores. Mateo and the other seminarians were assigned to clean the chapel, scrubbing the stone floors and polishing the brass candlesticks until they shone. The work was demanding, but it offered a kind of simple satisfaction—at least, it usually did. That day, however, Mateo found himself paired with Tomás, who had been in a foul mood since morning. The older seminarian's patience seemed to have worn thin, and he snapped at Mateo more than once for moving too slowly or missing a spot.

At first, Mateo tried to brush it off, focusing on the rhythmic motion of his scrubbing brush. But as Tomás's temper flared again, Mateo's own frustration bubbled to the surface. They were in the middle of polishing the altar when Tomás made another sharp comment, and before Mateo knew it, he had snapped back, his voice carrying an edge he had not intended.

"Maybe if you weren't so busy criticizing, you'd see that I'm doing my best," Mateo muttered, more to himself than to Tomás, but the older seminarian heard him clearly.

Tomás turned, his expression darkening. "Watch your tone, Mateo. You think you're the only one struggling here? You think you're the only one who has doubts?"

The words hit Mateo harder than he expected. He felt a rush of anger mixed with shame, and for a moment he wanted to shout back, to let all his frustrations spill out. But then he saw the weariness in Tomás's eyes, the deep lines of exhaustion that he had never noticed before. And suddenly, Mateo understood that the anger wasn't truly about him—it was about something deeper, something that Tomás, too, was wrestling with in the silence between the bell's tolls.

Mateo took a step back, forcing himself to take a deep breath. "I'm sorry, Tomás," he said quietly, the words coming out rough around the edges. "I didn't mean to take it out on you. I know we're all going through... something."

Tomás's expression softened, and for a moment, they stood there in the dimly lit chapel, two young men caught in the crosscurrents of their own uncertainties. Then, without another word, they returned to their work, the tension between them easing into a kind of unspoken understanding.

That night, as Mateo lay in his narrow bed, listening to the quiet breathing of the others, he thought about what Father Alvarez had said. He thought about the trials he had faced—both the ones he could name and the ones that remained hidden in the recesses of his heart. He realized that perhaps his time in the seminary wasn't meant to provide easy answers but to teach him how to live with the questions, how to endure the trials without losing sight of the faith that had brought him here in the first place.

The bell rang early the next morning, calling them to prayer, and for the first time in a while, Mateo felt a sense of acceptance settle over him. He didn't have the answers yet, and he knew that more trials lay ahead, but he also knew that he was not facing them alone. He had his fellow seminarians, his teachers, and the steady rhythm of the bell to guide him through the darkness. And maybe, just maybe, that would be enough to carry him forward.

CHAPTER 7

Lessons in Humility

The seminary days settled into a routine that might have felt monotonous to some, but for Mateo, every moment was an invitation to confront the tangled web of thoughts and doubts that had followed him from San Agustin. Each time the bell rang, he felt the familiar push and pull—a sense of belonging and yet a persistent feeling of being an outsider in his own heart. He came to understand that the seminary's rhythms, though demanding, were meant to do more than just fill the hours. They were designed to shape the soul, to wear away the rough edges like a river smooths a stone.

Of all the virtues the seminarians were taught, humility was the most emphasized and perhaps the most elusive. It was embedded in everything they did—from the way they were instructed to bow their heads in prayer to how they served one another in silence during meals. They learned that humility was not about thinking less of oneself but thinking of oneself less, a distinction that Mateo found more difficult to embody than he had imagined.

The lesson truly came to life for him on a rainy autumn morning, when the sky was overcast and the seminary grounds turned to muddy slush beneath their feet. The bell rang early, summoning them to their chores before the morning classes began. Mateo was assigned to clean the refectory with a group of other seminarians, including Diego and Emilio. The task seemed simple enough—scrubbing the floors, wiping down tables, and clearing away the remnants of the previous night's meal. But as they worked, a small accident sparked a lesson Mateo would carry with him for a long time.

Diego, carrying a large pot of water, slipped on the slick floor and sent the entire pot clattering to the ground. The water splashed everywhere, soaking their robes and turning the floor into a mess of muddy streaks. For a moment, there was silence, broken only by the sound of the rain outside and Diego's muttered curses.

Mateo knelt quickly, helping Diego gather the pot and the scattered rags. He offered a reassuring smile, trying to lighten the mood. "It's just water, hermano. We'll clean it up."

But Diego's expression remained tense, his face flushed with embarrassment. "It's my fault," he muttered, his voice tinged with frustration. "I should have been more careful. Now we'll be late for class, and Brother Domingo will have our heads."

Mateo glanced at Emilio, who was already starting to mop up the mess, his usual easy smile nowhere to be seen. He could sense the frustration simmering beneath the surface, the weight of their rigid schedule pressing down on them. They were all tired, worn thin by the unrelenting demands of seminary life, and Diego's mishap felt like one mistake too many.

As Mateo bent to help them, he felt something shift inside him—a realization that perhaps this moment, this small inconvenience, was not just another test of patience. It was a chance to practice what they had been taught day in and day out.

"Let's clean the room together," Mateo said, looking Diego in the eye. "It doesn't matter if we're a little late. We'll explain it to Brother Domingo, and he'll understand. We're all in this together, aren't we?"

Diego hesitated, his hands tightening around the mop handle, but then he let out a breath and nodded. Emilio joined in without a word, and together they began to wipe up the water, working silently but with a renewed sense of focus. Mateo found himself absorbed in the simple, repetitive motions—pressing the mop against the floor, wringing out the water, and scrubbing away the mud. The world seemed to narrow down to this small act, the rhythm of their movements falling into sync like a quiet prayer.

As they worked, Mateo realized that humility was not just about accepting one's flaws or learning to bow before God. It was also about accepting the imperfections in others, about finding grace in moments when frustration could easily take over. He thought of the lessons Father Alvarez had shared about the saints, who had served others in the most mundane ways—cooking meals, tending to the sick, washing feet—and he understood, perhaps for the first time, why those small acts of service were so revered.

When they finally finished cleaning the refectory, the bell rang again, and they hurried to their morning class, their robes still damp but their spirits lighter. Brother Domingo gave them a stern glance when they arrived late, but he said nothing about their appearance. As they settled into their seats,

Mateo caught Diego's eye, and they exchanged a small, understanding nod. It wasn't a grand gesture, but it felt like a step forward—a reminder that they were learning together, even in their stumbles.

The incident lingered in Mateo's thoughts throughout the week. He found himself noticing the little ways in which humility played out around him—in the way Tomás stayed behind after meals to help wash the dishes, or how Emilio gave up his spare time to tutor a struggling seminarian in Latin. These were the small, quiet sacrifices that no one celebrated but that carried a weight all their own. And they made Mateo wonder how he might do the same, how he could let go of his own pride and need for answers, and learn to serve without expectation.

The real test came a few days later, during one of their evening prayer sessions. The rain had returned, drumming against the stained-glass windows of the chapel, and the air was thick with the scent of damp wood and candle smoke. As they knelt in prayer, Mateo felt his mind wandering again, drifting back to San Agustin and the questions that still gnawed at him. He tried to focus on the psalms, to let the familiar words carry him into a state of peace, but his thoughts were restless, circling back to the doubts he could not shake.

When the prayers ended and the seminarians began to file out, Mateo stayed behind, staring up at the crucifix that hung over the altar. He thought of his father, who never showed any positive indication about his decision to enter the seminary. He felt a deep emptiness in his heart due to his father's reluctance. He reflected on how he had attempted to shoulder that burden, even when he lacked the strength to do so himself. And he thought of how, in a way, he had run from that weight when he chose to join the seminary, hoping that a life of service would somehow fill the emptiness he could not name.

Lost in thought, Mateo didn't notice Father Alvarez entering the chapel until he spoke. "You seem deep in contemplation, Mateo."

Mateo started, then offered the priest a sheepish smile. "I was just... thinking, Father. About humility, and why it's so difficult to truly live it."

Father Alvarez approached, his footsteps echoing softly in the empty chapel. He stood beside Mateo, his gaze fixed on the crucifix. "Humility is not just a virtue, Mateo. It is a surrender—a recognition that we are small in the face of God's mystery and that our understanding will always be limited. But that surrender is not meant to diminish us. It's meant to make us open, to create space within us where grace can enter."

Mateo nodded, absorbing the words, but his thoughts remained tangled. "I think…I've been trying to understand too much. I have been trying to find answers for everything, including things I'm not ready to face.

Father Alvarez turned to him then, his expression softening. "The answers will come in their time, Mateo. But for now, focus on being present. Trust that the small acts, the quiet moments, and the lessons learned through service—they are all shaping you in ways you cannot yet see."

They stood together in silence, the rain a steady rhythm outside, the chapel filled with the glow of candlelight. And for the first time in a long while, Mateo felt a sense of release, as though a knot within him had begun to loosen. He realized that perhaps, in this journey, it was enough to simply be—to listen, to serve, and to wait for the understanding that would come when it was meant to.

As he left the chapel, the bell rang again, calling the seminarians to bed. Mateo walked toward the dormitory, feeling the damp air cool against his skin, and he thought of the work yet to be done, of the trials that still awaited him. But he also thought of the small moments of grace he had witnessed, the quiet strength of his fellow seminarians, and the unexpected lessons they had taught him.

For the first time, Mateo allowed himself to hope that perhaps he could find peace here—not in grand revelations, but in the humility of daily life, in the steady rhythm of the bell, and in the companionship of those who walked this path with him. And though he did not yet have all the answers, he knew that he was learning to carry the questions with a little more grace.

CHAPTER 8

Spiritual Growth

The winter months crept in slowly, bringing with them a deep cold that settled into the stone walls of the seminary. Frost coated the windows each morning, and the breath of the seminarians lingered in the air as they made their way to the chapel for morning prayers. Despite the chill that seeped into their bones, there was a quiet beauty in the way the seminary grounds transformed. The trees stood bare and proud, their branches latticed against a sky that was often a pale, clear blue. And through it all, the bell continued its steadfast rhythm, guiding their days like a metronome of faith.

For Mateo, the cold seemed to sharpen his thoughts, like a blade being honed. The doubts that had once clouded his mind began to settle into a clearer form, their edges more defined but less overwhelming. He began to find comfort in the routine of his studies and prayers, even as he wrestled with the deeper questions that refused to let go. There was something in the starkness of winter that mirrored his own inner landscape—a stripping away of excess, a search for the essence of what lay beneath.

The seminary's library became a refuge during these months, a place where Mateo could lose himself in the ancient texts and writings of the Church fathers. He spent long hours poring over the words of Augustine, Aquinas, and the mystics who had sought to describe the ineffable. He was particularly drawn to the writings of St. John of the Cross, whose poetry spoke of a *dark night of the soul,* a period of spiritual desolation that ultimately led to a deeper union with God.

As he read, Mateo couldn't help but feel a kinship with the saint's words. He understood what it meant to walk through darkness, to seek the light even when it seemed distant and dim. And yet, St. John's writings offered a promise that Mateo had not considered before—that the darkness itself could be a part of God's plan, a necessary passage through which the soul must travel to reach true understanding.

One afternoon, as snowflakes drifted softly past the library windows, Mateo found himself lost in thought, a passage from *The Ascent of Mount Carmel* open before him. *To reach satisfaction in all, desire its possession in nothing. To come to the knowledge of all, desire the knowledge of nothing.* The words seemed to echo in his mind, reverberating through the quiet corners of his heart.

"Mateo, you'll freeze if you stay here much longer."

Emilio's voice broke through the stillness, and Mateo looked up to see his friend standing in the doorway, his cheeks flushed from the cold outside. Emilio shook his head with a half-amused smile, stepping inside and closing the door behind him.

"Honestly, hermano, I think you spend more time with those dusty books than with the rest of us. You should come join us by the fire. It's warmer there, and we could all use a bit of company."

Mateo hesitated, glancing down at the book in his hands, but then he closed it gently and rose to follow Emilio. There was a time when he might have shied away from the camaraderie of his fellow seminarians, preferring the solitude of his thoughts, but lately he had begun to understand the value of their companionship. They were all walking the same path, even if their steps sometimes faltered. And in their shared struggles, Mateo found a kind of fellowship that eased the loneliness he carried.

They joined a small group gathered around the hearth in the common room, the fire crackling as the flames cast dancing shadows across the stone walls. Tomás was there, as always, his broad shoulders hunched forward as he listened to the conversations unfolding around him. Diego, too, had joined the group, his usually serious expression softened by the warmth of the fire. They spoke of their studies, of the latest sermons they had heard, and of the challenges they faced in trying to live out the virtues they read about in scripture.

At some point, the conversation turned to the nature of faith itself—a topic that was never far from their minds, yet one that carried a special weight during these dark winter months. Diego spoke first, his voice thoughtful as he leaned back in his chair.

"It's strange, isn't it? How we're taught that faith should be like a rock, something solid and unchanging, and yet... it often feels more like water, slipping through your hands when you try to hold on too tightly."

Tomás nodded in agreement, his gaze distant. "Faith is not static. It grows; it changes, just as we do. I think sometimes we forget that even the saints had their doubts, their moments of darkness. That's what makes their faith so remarkable—that they continued to seek God even when He seemed hidden."

Mateo listened, the flames casting a warm glow on his face, and he found himself speaking before he had fully formed the words. "Maybe that's why it's called a journey, not a destination. We're meant to walk through the darkness, to question, to struggle. It's part of what shapes us."

His words surprised even himself, and for a moment, the room fell silent. The others turned to look at him, their expressions reflecting a mixture of curiosity and understanding. Mateo felt a sudden vulnerability, as if he had exposed a part of himself that he wasn't yet ready to face. But then Emilio clapped him on the shoulder, breaking the tension with a laugh.

"Look at you, turning into a philosopher, Mateo! I thought I was the only one who liked to get lost in these kinds of thoughts."

The laughter that followed was warm and genuine, and Mateo found himself smiling despite the unease that still lingered beneath the surface. He realized that perhaps, in speaking his thoughts aloud, he had taken a small step forward, a step toward accepting the uncertainties that had haunted him since the day he arrived.

As the evening wore on, the conversation shifted to lighter topics, and the seminarians shared stories from their hometowns, their laughter mingling with the crackling of the fire. But even as they joked and reminisced, Mateo felt a quiet sense of growth within him, as if something deep inside had begun to shift. It was not a grand revelation but a small flicker of understanding, a sense that maybe the darkness he feared was not an obstacle but a part of the path he was meant to walk.

Later that night, as he returned to the dormitory, Mateo paused outside the chapel, listening to the muffled sound of the wind against the windows. He thought of the saints who had walked through their own dark nights and of the quiet strength he had seen in his fellow seminarians. And he thought of the words he had read earlier that day—about desiring nothing, about letting go of the need for certainty.

He knelt in the chapel, the cold stone pressing against his knees, and for the first time, he prayed not for answers, but for the grace to embrace the mystery. He prayed for the courage to walk through the dark without demanding a light, to trust that God was present even when His voice seemed distant. And as the bell rang softly in the distance, signaling the hour, Mateo felt a small peace settle over him, like a blanket against the winter chill.

The days that followed were no easier, but they were different. Mateo began to see his studies not as a search for definitive answers, but as an exploration—an opportunity to deepen his understanding of a God who could not be contained within the pages of a book. He approached his prayers with a new openness, allowing himself to sit with the silence rather than filling it with words. And in the stillness, he began to hear echoes that he had not noticed before—the gentle stirrings of hope, the faint whisper of a promise that he could not yet name.

The seminary remained a place of trials, of struggles and setbacks, but Mateo began to understand that growth did not always come in a straight line. It was a slow, winding journey, one that required patience and a willingness to be shaped by each step along the way. And though he knew there would be more darkness to face, he also knew that he did not walk through it alone.

In the company of his fellow seminarians, in the quiet wisdom of Father Alvarez, and in the steady rhythm of the bell, Mateo found the strength to continue. And as winter deepened around them, he began to see that perhaps, beneath the snow and the frozen earth, new growth was already beginning, waiting for the warmth that would come with spring.

CHAPTER 9

A Glimpse of the Divine

Winter wrapped its fingers tightly around the seminary, and the days grew shorter, the sky often remaining a steely gray from dawn until dusk. Snow piled high along the edges of the courtyard, muffling the world in a blanket of silence that made the ringing of the bell sound even more resonant, like a voice calling out across an empty landscape. Inside the seminary, the heat from the fireplaces struggled to warm the stone halls, and the seminarians wrapped themselves in their thick robes, gathering wherever they could find even a trace of warmth.

For Mateo, the cold only seemed to amplify the inner chill that had taken root within him, a numbness that made him feel as if he was moving through the days in a fog. He went through the motions—attending classes, joining the prayers, performing his duties—but there was a sense that something essential was slipping away from him, like water through his cupped hands. Even his conversations with Emilio and Tomás felt distant, as if he were watching himself from somewhere far outside his own body.

It was during this time that the seminary announced a spiritual retreat—a week of silence and meditation to draw the seminarians deeper into their prayer life. They would leave the structured schedule of classes behind and spend their days in the forested retreat center a few miles away, where the only sounds would be the wind through the trees and the distant murmurs of the river that wound its way through the hills.

Father Alvarez spoke of the retreat as an opportunity to encounter God in a more personal way, to let the distractions of daily life fall away and open themselves to the presence of the divine. But as the seminarians gathered their things and prepared for the journey, Mateo could not help but feel a sense of dread coiling within him, like a cold knot in his stomach. He worried that the silence would not bring him closer to God but instead expose the hollowness he felt growing inside him, the doubts that he had managed to keep at bay with the noise of everyday life.

The retreat center was a small, simple building nestled among a grove of ancient pines, their branches heavy with snow. The air was crisp and clean, tinged with the scent of evergreen, and the ground crunched beneath their boots as they walked the path toward the chapel. The center had no electricity, no modern comforts—only wooden benches, a stone hearth, and a single candle that burned on the altar of the tiny chapel. Father Alvarez lit the candle on their first evening there, its flickering light creating a long shadow over the rough-hewn walls.

"This week, we will speak only to God," he said, his voice hushed but firm, as if the very air in the chapel demanded reverence. "Let your hearts be open to whatever He might reveal to you, whether it is joy or sorrow, clarity or confusion. Trust that even in the silence, He is near."

With that, the retreat began. Each day followed the same pattern—waking with the dawn, gathering in the chapel for silent prayer, then scattering throughout the forest to spend the hours in quiet reflection. Meals were taken in solitude, each seminarian finding a spot to sit and eat their simple rations while contemplating the landscape around them.

At first, the silence was unbearable for Mateo. His thoughts seemed to echo endlessly in the stillness, bouncing off the walls of his mind like trapped birds. He found himself replaying memories of San Agustin, the faces of the townspeople flashing through his mind—his mother's tired smile, the old men sitting outside the café, and the children playing by the riverbanks. He thought of the promises he had made, the responsibilities he had left behind, and the questions that had driven him to seek refuge in the seminary.

He tried to focus on the prayers he had memorized, to let the familiar words steady him, but even those seemed to slip away like mist. Each time he closed his eyes, he saw the river in his mind's eye, its waters flowing swiftly beneath a sky darkening with the onset of winter. He felt as if he were standing on its banks once more, caught between the desire to move forward and the pull of everything he had left behind.

But then, something shifted.

It was on the fourth day of the retreat, when the sun emerged unexpectedly from behind the clouds, casting a golden light over the snow-covered trees. Mateo had wandered deeper into the woods than before, drawn by a path that wound through the pines toward the river. The air was still, save for the occasional creak of the trees as they shifted under the weight of the snow, and Mateo found himself pausing beside the riverbank, staring at the water as it flowed beneath a thin sheet of ice.

He knelt down, resting his hands on the frost-covered earth, and closed his eyes, letting the sound of the river fill his ears. For the first time since the retreat began, he stopped trying to force his thoughts into order. He let them flow as freely as the river, allowing himself to feel the full weight of his uncertainty, his sorrow, and his fear. He offered no words, no petitions, only the raw, unspoken desires of his heart—the desire to understand, to be understood, and to find a sense of peace that he had long believed was beyond his reach.

In that moment, something unexpected happened. It was not a voice, not a vision, but a feeling—a presence that settled over him like the warmth of the sun on a winter's day. Mateo felt a sudden rush of clarity, a deep, overwhelming sense of being seen, as if a veil had been lifted from his eyes. It was as if the river, the trees, and the very ground beneath him were alive, with a hidden life, a life that pulsed with the rhythm of his own heartbeat. And in that pulse, he felt something that he had not felt in a long time: hope.

Tears filled his eyes, unbidden and uncontrollable, and he let them fall into the snow, his breath catching in his chest. He did not understand what he had encountered, but for the first time, he did not need to understand. He felt his heart open in a way he had not thought possible, a release that came with no words, only the sense that he was being held in the presence of something infinitely greater than himself. It was a glimpse of the divine, as fleeting and as powerful as the sun breaking through the clouds.

When he finally opened his eyes, the light had shifted, creating long shadows that covered the snow. Mateo stood slowly, feeling the cold bite into his skin, but there was a warmth in his chest that the winter air could not touch. He walked back to the retreat center with a sense of quiet awe, as if he had just awoken from a dream that lingered even in waking.

The rest of the retreat passed in a blur. Mateo did not speak of what he had experienced, not even to Father Alvarez when they returned to the seminary. It felt too fragile, too sacred, to be reduced to words. But he carried it with him, like a small flame burning in the depths of his heart, a reminder that even in his darkest moments, he was not alone.

When they returned to the seminary, the routine of classes and prayers resumed, but Mateo approached each day with a new sense of purpose. The questions he had carried with him did not vanish, nor did the doubts that had plagued him. But he no longer saw them as barriers; instead, he saw them as part of the path he was walking, a path that led not away from his struggles but through them.

One evening, Emilio joined Mateo outside the chapel, where Mateo stood watching the snow fall softly against the darkening sky, his breath forming small clouds in the frigid air.

"You seem... different, Mateo," Emilio said quietly, glancing at his friend with a curious expression. "More at peace. Did something happen during the retreat?"

Mateo considered the question, feeling the weight of the secret he held in his heart. He thought of the river, of the warmth he had felt that day, and he offered Emilio a small, enigmatic smile. "Maybe," he said softly. "Or maybe I just learned to listen a little better."

Emilio raised an eyebrow, but he did not press for more. They stood together in companionable silence, watching the snow fall in the glow of the chapel's windows. And as the bell rang, calling them to evening prayer, Mateo found himself whispering a prayer of gratitude—a prayer not for answers, but for the mystery that had brought him this far, and for the small, flickering light that guided his way through the darkness.

CHAPTER 10

A Crisis of Faith

The days following the retreat were marked by a newfound clarity, a quiet sense of peace that Mateo carried with him like a warm ember against the winter's chill. The memory of his encounter by the river stayed with him, a small but steady light that guided him through the routine of seminary life. Yet, as the weeks passed, the challenges he had thought he had overcome began to return, creeping back into the corners of his mind like shadows stretching in the fading light.

The winter grew harsher, blanketing the seminary in a deeper cold. The chapel felt like a tomb at times, its stone floors icy even beneath the thick robes these seminarians wore. The bell, ever constant, rang through the snow-filled air, but its sound felt different to Mateo—less like a call to prayer and more like a reminder of the uncertainties that still clung to him. He began to wonder if the peace he had found during the retreat was merely a brief respite, a mirage that had faded now that he had returned to the grind of daily life.

One evening, after a particularly grueling day of study, Mateo found himself in the seminary library, surrounded by books he had once found comforting but that now seemed to mock him with their heavy, unchanging truths. The words on the pages blurred before his eyes, and he closed the volume with a frustrated sigh, the sound echoing in the otherwise empty room.

He pressed his palms against his eyes, feeling a familiar heaviness settle into his chest—a feeling he had come to know as the first stirrings of doubt. He tried to pray, but the words felt hollow, as if they were slipping through his fingers before they could reach God's ears. He thought of the river from the retreat, of the warmth he had felt, but even that memory seemed distant, like a dream he could no longer recall in detail.

As the minutes passed, Mateo's frustration grew. He wondered if he had been fooling himself all along, if the sense of purpose he had felt during the retreat was just a product of wishful thinking. He wondered if he truly belonged here at all.

That night, as he lay in bed, the doubts continued to swirl around him, like a storm gathering strength. The sound of the bell echoed in his mind, its steady rhythm clashing with the frantic pace of his thoughts. He turned over in his narrow bunk, staring up at the shadows that flickered across the ceiling, and felt a sharp pang of fear—fear that he had come this far only to discover that he did not have the faith he had thought he did.

The crisis came to a head a few days later, during one of their theology classes with Father Alvarez. They were discussing the nature of grace and free will, a subject that had always fascinated Mateo. But today, the discussion felt like a weight pressing down on his chest, each argument and counterargument only deepening his sense of confusion.

Tomás, who often spoke with a quiet confidence, was in the midst of making a point about how grace could coexist with human suffering when Mateo found himself interrupting, his voice sharper than he intended. "But how do we know?" he blurted out, drawing surprised looks from his classmates. "How do we know that grace is real, that it's not just something we tell ourselves to make sense of the world's suffering?"

The room fell silent, all eyes turning toward him. Tomás's brow furrowed in confusion, and even Father Alvarez seemed taken aback by the sudden outburst. Mateo felt his face flush with heat, but he pressed on, unable to keep the words from spilling out.

"I mean, we talk about grace as if it's some kind of light that we can all feel, but what if we're wrong? What if it's just... just a story we tell ourselves to make everything seem less meaningless?" His voice broke slightly, and he quickly looked down at his hands, realizing too late how exposed he had made himself.

Father Alvarez regarded him for a long moment, his expression unreadable. Then he gestured for the other students to leave, while keeping his gaze fixed on Mateo. The seminarians filed out, casting Mateo concerned glances as they went, but he barely noticed. He could feel his heart pounding in his chest, his breath coming in shallow bursts, as if he had just run a great distance.

When they were alone, Father Alvarez leaned forward, folding his hands together on the desk. "You are not the first to have these doubts, Mateo," he said softly, his voice devoid of judgment. "And you will not be the last. But I need you to tell me what has brought you to this moment. What is it that you fear?"

The question cut through Mateo's defenses, and he felt something inside him crack. He took a deep, shuddering breath, trying to steady himself, but the words tumbled out in a rush. "I don't know if I believe anymore," he confessed, his voice barely more than a whisper. "I thought I did. I thought I had found some kind of peace. But now... now it all feels so far away. Like I'm trying to grasp at smoke."

Father Alvarez remained silent, letting the words hang in the air between them. Then he rose from his seat and walked to the window, looking out at the snow-covered courtyard where the other seminarians had gathered for their afternoon chores.

"Faith is not a straight path, Mateo," he said after a moment, his tone thoughtful. "It is a winding road, one that often leads us through dark valleys before we can find the light again. You are in one of those valleys now, and it is painful. But that does not mean you have lost your way."

Mateo shook his head, his frustration boiling over. "But what if I can't find my way back? What if I'm just... empty inside?"

Father Alvarez turned to face him, his expression gentle but firm. "Then let the emptiness be your prayer. Let your doubts be your offering. God does not ask for perfect faith, Mateo. He asks for an open heart—a heart that is willing to seek Him, even when He seems absent."

The words struck something deep within Mateo, and he felt a sudden surge of emotion rise in his throat. He looked down at his hands, the hands that had held the scriptures, that had grasped the rosary beads, that had served and labored, and he wondered if he had ever truly opened them, if he had ever truly surrendered his need for control.

"I don't know how," he admitted finally, his voice cracking. "I don't know how to trust that He's there."

Father Alvarez's expression softened, and he placed a hand on Mateo's shoulder. "None of us do, not completely. That is why we keep seeking. That is why we keep listening for His voice, even when all we hear is silence."

They stood together in the quiet of the classroom, the snow falling softly outside the window, and for the first time in a long while, Mateo allowed himself to feel the weight of his own vulnerability. He realized that he had been trying to carry the burden of certainty alone, clinging to the idea that faith meant having all the answers. But now, he saw that perhaps faith was more like a wound—something that ached, that bled, but that could also heal with time.

In the days that followed, Mateo continued to struggle. The doubts did not vanish; they lingered like shadows on the edge of his vision. But he began to approach them differently—not as enemies to be banished, but as companions on the journey, reminders that he was human, that he was still growing, still learning what it meant to believe.

He found himself returning to the chapel late at night, kneeling in the darkness and listening to the sound of his own breathing. He did not pray for answers but simply let the silence wash over him, allowing himself to be present in the uncertainty. And slowly, he began to sense a change—not a dramatic revelation, but a quiet shift, like the first hint of dawn breaking over the snow-covered hills.

The bell continued to ring, marking each new day, and every new moment of struggle and surrender. And as Mateo moved through the seminary's halls, as he shared his doubts with Emilio and Tomás and listened to their own confessions, he realized that he was not alone in his crisis. They were all searching, all stumbling in the darkness, but they were searching together.

And perhaps, Mateo thought, as he listened to the bell's steady toll, that was the beginning of faith—not a certainty that dispelled the shadows, but a willingness to walk through them, trusting that somewhere beyond the darkness, the light would come.

Chapter II

Acts of Compassion

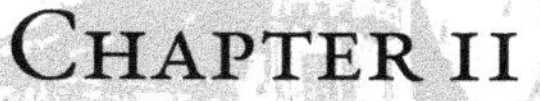

The new year arrived quietly, the heavy snows giving way to a brittle cold that stretched across the seminary grounds like a blanket. The days lengthened, and though the trees still stood bare against the gray sky, there was a sense of change in the air, a promise that spring would eventually come to melt away the frost. Within the seminary, the routines continued—classes, prayers, manual labor—but Mateo found himself yearning for something beyond the walls that had become so familiar to him.

It was during one of their morning lectures that Father Alvarez announced a new initiative. The parish nearby had been struggling to provide for the community's poorest members, many of whom were suffering through the harsh winter without enough food or warmth. The seminary was being called upon to assist, to extend their work of prayer into a work of action. Father Alvarez's voice, as he spoke to the seminarians, carried a gravity that made each word feel like a commandment.

"We are not called to live apart from the world, but to serve it," he reminded them, his eyes scanning the room. "It is easy to study the teachings of Christ in the warmth of this classroom, but far harder to live them in the cold streets. This trip will be an opportunity for you to see firsthand what it means to be a servant, to bring compassion to those who need it most. I hope you will embrace this chance with open hearts."

Mateo listened intently, a quiet excitement building within him. For months, he had felt as if he were turning inward, consumed by his own doubts and uncertainties, but this seemed like a chance to reach beyond himself, to see if he could find God's presence not just in the silence of the chapel but in the faces of those who suffered. He volunteered eagerly when the time came, joining a group of seminarians that included Tomás, Diego, and Emilio.

The next day, they left the seminary in the early hours, the sun still hidden behind a veil of clouds.

They piled into a rickety old van, its heater sputtering in the cold, and drove down the winding roads to the nearby town. Mateo sat by the window, watching as the landscape shifted from snow-covered fields to rows of modest houses with smoke rising from their chimneys. The town reminded him of San Agustin in some ways—small, close-knit, and worn at the edges by years of hardship.

Their destination was a small parish that served as both a place of worship and a makeshift shelter for those in need. As they arrived, they were greeted by Father José, an elderly priest with a kind, weathered face and hands that seemed too large for his thin frame. Despite his age, he moved with a tireless energy, guiding the seminarians through the tasks that awaited them.

They spent the morning sorting through donations—blankets, canned food, warm clothing—and organizing them into packages for distribution. Mateo found a kind of satisfaction in the work, the simplicity of folding clothes and stacking boxes a welcome relief from the more abstract challenges of his studies. He worked alongside Tomás, who carried the heavier loads without complaint, and Diego, who carefully sorted the donations with a precision that reflected his nature.

But it was when they began to distribute the packages that Mateo felt the true weight of their task. The people who came to the parish were as varied as the town itself—elderly men and women with faces lined by years of toil, young mothers clutching their children close, and those who had fallen through the cracks of society, their eyes carrying the haunted look of lives lived on the margins. Mateo handed out food and blankets with a quiet smile, offering words of comfort where he could, but he could not help but feel a pang of sadness each time he met their gaze.

One man, in particular, stayed with him. He was middle-aged, his hair unkempt and his coat threadbare. He approached Mateo with a shy, almost apologetic expression, as if asking for help was a shameful act. Mateo offered him a bundle of supplies, and the man took it with trembling hands, his eyes welling with gratitude.

"Thank you," the man murmured, his voice rough from the cold. "I don't know what I'd do without this. It's been... a hard winter."

Mateo nodded, unsure of what to say. He thought of the theological arguments they had debated in class, the careful distinctions they drew between charity and justice, grace and works. But here, standing in the cold with this man who had so little, those distinctions felt far away and abstract. All that mattered was the need before him and the simple act of meeting it.

"You're welcome," Mateo said finally, his voice gentle. "We're here to help, however we can."

The man nodded, his expression softening, and for a moment, their eyes met—two strangers sharing a moment of connection in the midst of their very different lives. Mateo watched as the man turned and walked back toward the street, clutching the bundle tightly to his chest, and he felt a warmth bloom within him, like a small fire kindled against the winter wind.

As the day wore on, the seminarians worked tirelessly, handing out supplies and offering hot soup to those who came seeking warmth. Mateo's body ached with fatigue, but he found himself smiling more than he had in weeks, a genuine joy that came from the simple act of serving others. He saw the same joy reflected in his companions—Emilio's laughter as he entertained the children, Diego's careful attention to detail as he prepared each package, and even Tomás's usually somber face softened by a rare, quiet smile.

By the time the sun dipped low in the sky, casting long shadows across the snow-covered streets, their work was nearly done. Father José gathered them in the parish hall, his voice filled with gratitude as he thanked them for their efforts. "You have done good work today," he said, his eyes crinkling at the corners. "Remember that compassion is not just a gift we give to others; it is a gift we receive ourselves. In serving others, we draw closer to the heart of Christ."

The words lingered in Mateo's mind as they made their way back to the van, the town growing dark behind them. He sat in the back seat, watching the lights of the houses flicker by, and he felt a strange, bittersweet ache in his chest. He thought of the faces he had seen that day—faces filled with gratitude, with weariness, with hope—and he realized that something had shifted inside him.

It was as if he had caught a glimpse of a different kind of faith, a faith that was not confined to the chapel or the pages of scripture but that lived in the everyday acts of kindness, in the shared warmth of a blanket, and in the small, unspoken moments of connection. It was a faith that required him to be present, see humanity in others, and let himself be seen in return.

That night, as he lay in his bunk back at the seminary, Mateo found himself praying again, but this time his prayer was not for understanding or certainty. It was a prayer of gratitude—for the chance to serve, for the chance to see beyond himself, and for the hope that maybe, just maybe, he was finding a way forward.

He did not know where this path would lead or if he would ever find the answers he sought. But as the bell rang in the distance, calling the seminary to sleep, Mateo felt a quiet resolve settle over him. He understood now that faith was not something he could possess or master; it was something he could only live, one small act of compassion at a time.

And perhaps, in those small acts, he was beginning to find a deeper connection to the God he had been searching for all along—a God who was not found in grand revelations, but in the quiet, persistent call to love and serve the least among them.

CHAPTER 12

The Weight of Responsibility

As winter's grip began to loosen, the days grew lighter, and a subtle warmth returned to the seminary grounds. The first hints of spring revealed themselves in the buds on the trees and the thawing earth beneath the snow. But with this change in season came a shift in the atmosphere within the seminary—a sense of urgency, of preparation for what lay ahead.

For Mateo, the transition from winter to spring felt like a shifting tide, carrying with it new challenges and responsibilities. The seminary's curriculum intensified as they approached the Lenten season. It was a time for reflection and penitence, but also a time when the seminarians were expected to deepen their understanding of the sacramental life they would one day be entrusted with.

Father Alvarez had taken a particular interest in guiding Mateo during this time, perhaps sensing the lingering questions and uncertainties that still simmered beneath the surface. He began assigning Mateo to lead small prayer sessions with the younger seminarians, encouraging him to take on more responsibility within their community. It was a test, Mateo knew—a way to see if he could carry the weight of leadership, even in a limited capacity.

At first, Mateo approached these tasks with a sense of nervousness. Standing before his peers, leading them through prayers and readings, he felt exposed in a way he had never experienced before. It was one thing to pray silently in the chapel, with only God as his witness. It was another to speak words meant to guide others, knowing that they looked to him for direction.

One evening, as he prepared to lead a prayer session in the chapel, Mateo felt the familiar twist of anxiety in his chest. He stood at the front of the small gathering, his hands gripping the edges of the lectern, and tried to steady his breathing. The faces before him were kind and familiar—Emilio with his easygoing smile, Diego with his thoughtful eyes, and Tomás with his ever-present aura of quiet strength. However, the weight of their expectations pressed down on him, causing his mouth to become dry.

He began the session with a passage from the Gospel of Matthew, reading aloud the words that he had read so many times before. *"Come to me, all you who are weary and burdened, and I will give you rest. Take my yoke upon you and learn from me, for I am gentle and humble in heart, and you will find rest for your souls."*

As he spoke, he felt the words falter on his tongue, their meaning slipping away like sand through his fingers. He glanced up and saw that the seminarians were watching him intently, waiting for him to offer some insight, some interpretation that might bring the passage to life. But for the first time, Mateo felt acutely aware of how little he truly knew—how vast the gap was between the teachings he had studied and the lived reality of faith.

He took a deep breath, willing himself to continue. "These words... they're meant to comfort us, I think. To remind us that we don't carry our burdens alone. But sometimes... it's hard to believe that, isn't it? When the burdens feel so heavy."

Mateo's voice wavered, but he pressed on, feeling a strange mix of vulnerability and determination. "I know that many of us are struggling, in different ways. And I don't have all the answers. But I think... I think that maybe it's enough to know that Christ invites us to share those burdens with Him, even when we can't see the path clearly."

When the session ended, the seminarians dispersed with quiet words of thanks, but Mateo remained in the chapel, his hands still trembling from the effort. He knelt before the altar, bowing his head, and let out a breath he hadn't realized he'd been holding.

He wondered if he had done enough, if his words had reached anyone. He thought of the weight that Father Gabriel had carried in San Agustin, how the townspeople had looked to him for guidance in their moments of despair and uncertainty. Mateo had always admired that strength, but now, faced with even a fraction of that responsibility, he understood how heavy it could be.

He did not hear Father Alvarez enter the chapel, but he felt the older priest's presence beside him as he knelt.

"You did well tonight, Mateo," Father Alvarez said quietly, placing a gentle hand on Mateo's shoulder, his expression thoughtful but warm. "You spoke from the heart, and that is what matters most."

Mateo shook his head, struggling to find the right words for the turmoil inside him. "But I didn't say anything profound. I just... I just admitted that I don't have the answers. How can I guide others when I'm so uncertain myself?"

Father Alvarez's grip on his shoulder tightened slightly, a comforting weight. "True leadership is not about having all the answers, Mateo. It's about walking with others through their questions. The burden you feel—it is not yours to carry alone. It is meant to be shared with God and with those around you. You are not called to be perfect; rather, you are called to be honest.

The words settled into Mateo like small, unassuming seeds, but they were full of potential. He nodded slowly, allowing himself to absorb their meaning, even as doubt lingered at the edges of his thoughts. He had come to understand that the weight of responsibility was not just about the words he spoke but about the example he set, the way he lived out his faith in each small act of kindness and service. But still, he wondered if he was strong enough to carry that weight, to become the kind of priest that San Agustin's parish had looked to in Father Gabriel.

The following weeks were filled with similar moments, small but profound, that tested Mateo's ability to balance his role as a leader with his own ongoing journey of faith. He continued to lead the prayer sessions, each time finding a little more courage to speak openly about the struggles that had brought him to the seminary. He noticed that his honesty seemed to resonate with others—seminarians who had once seemed distant now approached him with their own doubts and fears, confiding in him as they walked together through the seminary grounds.

One cold morning, as they gathered in the common room to warm themselves by the fire, Emilio turned to Mateo with a thoughtful expression. "You know, Mateo, I think you're starting to find your voice," he said, a teasing smile playing on his lips. "Maybe you'll be the one delivering the homilies one day, giving us all a reason to stay awake during Mass."

Mateo laughed, but there was a part of him that still felt unworthy of such praise. He glanced over at Tomás, who was listening quietly from his place by the window. Tomás had always seemed so certain, so grounded in his faith, and Mateo often envied that steadiness. Yet, as their eyes met, Tomás gave him a small nod, a gesture of approval that meant more to Mateo than words could express.

But even as he found a measure of confidence, the weight of responsibility continued to press down on him, sometimes making it difficult to sleep at night. He thought often of the future, of the day when he would leave the seminary's walls and enter a parish of his own. He imagined standing before a congregation, feeling their expectations pressing down on him, and he wondered how he would find the strength to meet those expectations without losing himself.

On a particularly restless night, Mateo found himself wandering the seminary grounds, with the cold air biting at his cheeks. He walked until he reached the edge of the gardens, where the snow lay undisturbed, glowing faintly beneath the light of the moon. There, he paused, his breath rising in white clouds, and he looked up at the bell tower that loomed above him, its silhouette dark against the starlit sky.

The bell was silent now, resting between the calls that marked their days, but its presence was a reminder of the rhythms that governed their lives. Mateo had come to see the bell as a symbol of the constancy that the seminary offered—a constancy that he both relied on and resisted, wanting the freedom to chart his own course even as he feared what might lie beyond the comfort of routine.

He thought of the people he had met during their outreach in the nearby town—the man who had thanked him for a simple bundle of supplies and the children who had clung to Emilio's hand as they handed out food. He thought of their eyes, filled with a need so deep that no sermon or scripture could fully address it. And he realized that his fear was not just about his own uncertainties; it was about the responsibility of holding others' hopes, of becoming a source of light for those who looked to him in their darkness.

He knelt in the snow, bowing his head, and closed his eyes against the sting of the wind. "God, I don't know if I'm strong enough for this," he whispered, his voice barely more than a breath. "I don't know if I can bear the weight of so many lives. I thought I came here to find answers, but all I have are more questions."

For a long moment, there was only silence, the stillness of the night pressing in around him. But then, as if in response, he heard the faint sound of a door creaking open behind him. He turned to see Father Alvarez standing at the entrance of the chapel, wrapped in his long coat against the cold. The priest's face was shadowed, but there was a gentle smile in his voice as he spoke.

"Sometimes, God answers us in the silence, Mateo," Father Alvarez said, stepping out into the snow to join him. "But sometimes, He answers through the presence of those who walk beside us."

Mateo looked up, meeting the older man's eyes, and felt a sudden rush of gratitude. He had been so focused on his own struggles that he had forgotten the strength that could be found in the community, in the bonds he had formed with those who shared his path. He rose slowly, brushing the snow from his robes, and Father Alvarez clapped a hand on his shoulder.

"Come, let's go inside," the priest said, guiding him toward the warmth of the chapel. "It's too cold for soul-searching out here."

Inside the chapel, the air was warmer, carrying the faint scent of candles and incense. Father Alvarez led Mateo to a pew, and they sat together in the dim light, the silence between them no longer feeling like a void but like a space where something sacred might take root.

"Mateo," Father Alvarez began, his voice quiet but steady, "I know you fear the weight of the responsibility that comes with your calling. That is a fear that will never entirely leave you, even after you are ordained. But remember this: you are not called to save the world. You are called to love it—to love the people in your care, in their brokenness and their joy. The rest, you must leave to God."

Mateo closed his eyes, letting the words wash over him. He thought of the man in the town, of Tomás's quiet nod, of Emilio's easy laughter, of all the small moments of connection that had begun to fill the empty spaces within him. He thought of the way the bell called them to prayer each morning, not as a command but as an invitation, a reminder that each new day was a chance to serve, to be present, and to love.

He realized then that perhaps the weight he carried would never truly lift, but that he could learn to carry it with grace, with an open heart. Perhaps, in time, he would find the strength to hold both his own doubts and the hopes of others, to be a vessel that lets God's light shine through the cracks.

And as he knelt beside Father Alvarez in the quiet of the chapel, he whispered a prayer—not for the burden to be taken away, but for the courage to bear it and for the wisdom to see that he did not bear it alone.

Chapter 13

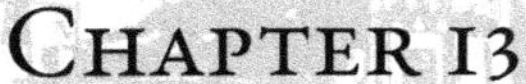

Love's Temptation

Spring came slowly to the seminary, thawing the last of the snow and bringing with it a damp warmth that clung to the air. The change in season was a welcome relief after the long, bitter winter, but it also brought a new restlessness to the seminary grounds. The seminarians, who had spent months bracing against the cold, now found themselves basking in the sun's pale light, lingering outdoors whenever their duties allowed. Laughter rang through the gardens as they turned the soil and planted new seeds, preparing for the growth that would follow the thaw.

But alongside this sense of renewal, Mateo found himself confronting a different kind of turmoil—one that he had not anticipated but that stirred within him with a force he could not ignore.

It began, as so many things did, in a seemingly innocent moment. One afternoon, as the seminarians gathered to help clear debris from the garden paths, they were joined by a group of volunteers from the nearby parish. Among them was a young woman named Clara, who had come with her mother to help prepare the grounds for the coming season. Clara was a few years younger than Mateo, with long brown hair that she kept tucked under a simple kerchief and a smile that seemed to light up even the dreariest of days.

Mateo had met Clara before, in passing, during one of the seminary's outreach events in town. But now, working side by side in the gardens, he saw her in a new light. They spoke as they worked, their conversations starting with the practicalities of gardening—how best to turn the soil, which seeds to plant where—but quickly drifting into more personal territory.

Clara spoke of her life in the parish, of her plans to study nursing at a nearby college, and of the small joys she found in everyday life—reading poetry by the river, walking the paths through the woods, and caring for the elderly members of her community. Mateo listened, drawn in by her warmth and her easy laughter, and found himself speaking more freely than he had in months.

He told her of his own struggles, the doubts that still lingered at the edges of his faith, and the unexpected challenges he faced in the seminary. He spoke of his hopes for the future, of the parish he imagined serving one day, and of the desire to make a difference in a world that often felt overwhelming in its need. Clara listened with a quiet attentiveness, her eyes never leaving his, and Mateo felt something shift inside him, like a door opening to a room he had not realized was there.

As the weeks passed, their conversations became a regular part of Mateo's routine. Clara continued to visit the seminary with her mother, bringing baskets of bread and preserves to share with the seminarians. Mateo found himself looking forward to her visits, lingering in the garden longer than necessary in the hope of catching a few minutes with her. Their talks became more intimate, the laughter softer, and the silences charged with an unspoken tension that both thrilled and unsettled him.

He knew, deep down, that he was treading dangerous ground. The seminary was a place of discipline, of strict adherence to vows and commitments, and Mateo's choice to pursue the priesthood meant embracing a life of celibacy, of turning away from the possibility of romantic love. He had accepted that choice when he entered the seminary, convinced that his calling required him to set aside such desires in favor of a greater devotion.

But Clara's presence stirred feelings he thought he had left behind in San Agustin—feelings of longing, of wanting to be seen and understood not just as a servant of God, but as a person. He began to dream of her, of the warmth of her hand in his, of her laughter echoing through the empty halls of the seminary. The dreams left him feeling guilty and confused, torn between his commitment to the path he had chosen and the desire for a different kind of connection.

One evening, as the sun dipped low in the sky and cast a golden glow across the courtyard, Mateo found himself sitting with Clara beneath a blooming cherry tree, the air fragrant with the scent of new blossoms. They had finished their work for the day, and Clara had brought a small loaf of sweet bread wrapped in cloth, which they shared in comfortable silence. Mateo watched her as she gazed out over the garden, her face softened by the evening light, and felt his chest tighten with an unfamiliar ache.

"Clara," he said quietly, breaking the silence, "I need to tell you something."

She turned to him, her expression curious but open, and Mateo hesitated, struggling to find the right words. He had rehearsed this conversation in his mind a dozen times, but now that the moment was here, his thoughts scattered like petals on the wind.

"I...I don't know how to say this without sounding foolish," he began, his voice unsteady. "But these past weeks, I've felt... something I didn't expect. Something that makes me question things I thought were certain."

Clara's smile faded, replaced by a look of concern. "Mateo, you don't have to explain. I know what your calling means to you. And I know that whatever you're feeling, it's not easy."

Mateo looked away, feeling the heat rise in his cheeks. He had hoped that speaking the words aloud might bring some relief, some clarity, but instead he felt only a deeper confusion, as if he were standing at the edge of a precipice, unsure whether to step forward or pull back.

"It's not just about the calling," he said, his voice barely more than a whisper. "It's about you. About how I feel when I'm with you. And I know I shouldn't feel this way, but..."

He trailed off, unable to finish the thought. Clara remained silent for a moment, her expression unreadable, and Mateo felt his heart sink, fearing that he had ruined whatever fragile connection they had built.

But then she reached out and placed a hand on his arm, her touch gentle but firm. "Mateo, I care about you too," she said softly, her eyes searching his. "But I think you already know what you need to do. You've made a choice—a choice that's brought you here, to this place, to this path. And I don't want to be the reason you turn away from that."

Mateo closed his eyes, feeling the sting of her words but also the truth in them. He had come to the seminary to dedicate himself to a higher calling, to serve a purpose greater than himself. Yet, he had allowed himself to be drawn into a different kind of longing, one that was no less real but that did not align with the life he had chosen.

He opened his eyes, meeting Clara's gaze, and saw the sadness there—the same sadness that mirrored his own. He knew then that she understood the struggle he faced, that she shared in the weight of his decision, even if it meant letting go of whatever might have grown between them.

"Clara, I—" he began, but she shook her head gently, stopping him.

"It's all right, Mateo," she said, offering him a sad, wistful smile. "You don't have to explain. Just promise me that whatever you decide, you'll do it with your whole heart. Don't let doubt hold you back, not in this, not in anything."

Mateo nodded, swallowing against the lump in his throat. He wanted to say more, to express the gratitude he felt for her understanding and the pain of the choice he was making, but the words would not come. Instead, he reached out and took her hand, holding it for a moment, feeling the warmth of her skin against his.

They sat together until the sun disappeared behind the trees, the sky darkening into twilight. And when it was time to part, they stood in silence, each knowing that this was a farewell of sorts, even if neither of them spoke the words aloud.

As Mateo watched Clara walk back toward the parish with her mother, her figure growing smaller in the distance, he felt a strange mixture of grief and relief. He knew that the path ahead would be difficult, that the feelings he had uncovered would not simply vanish overnight. But he also knew that he had made the right choice, that the ache in his chest was a part of learning what it meant to love without possession, to let go of something beautiful in order to remain true to the life he had chosen.

That night, as he knelt in the chapel, Mateo prayed for strength, for clarity, and for the courage to face the temptations that had tested him. He prayed for Clara, too, for her happiness and her future, and he asked God to help him carry the memory of their time together without letting it become a source of regret.

And as the bell rang, signaling the hour, Mateo felt a quiet resolve settle over him. He knew that this experience, painful as it was, had been another step on his journey—another lesson in what it meant to choose a life of service, a life of sacrifice. He had faced a part of himself that he had not wanted to see, but in facing it, he had found a deeper understanding of what his calling required.

He rose from his knees, the echoes of the bell fading into the night, and walked back toward the dormitory with a heart that was both heavier and lighter than before. And though he did not know what trials lay ahead, he knew that he would face them with a clearer sense of who he was and of the path he had chosen to walk.

As he walked back through the seminary's shadowed halls, the thoughts of his conversations with Clara lingered. Every step seemed to echo the weight of what he was leaving behind, but also the choice he had made. He understood that while love in its romantic form was a gift, it was not the gift he could accept, not if he wanted to remain true to the vows he had set his heart on. He thought of the times he had seen the older priests, men like Father Gabriel and Father Alvarez, carrying their own burdens of sacrifice with quiet dignity. He wondered if they too had faced temptations like this, moments that pulled them away from the path they had chosen.

In the dormitory, Mateo found that sleep did not come easily that night. He lay awake, the moonlight casting pale shapes on the walls, his mind filled with the memory of Clara's voice, her gentle understanding, and the bittersweet finality of their farewell. He replayed their conversation again and again, until the words blurred with the sound of the wind outside.

And yet, beneath the sorrow, there was a strange sense of peace—a recognition that his choice, difficult as it had been, was one he could live with. He realized that part of what made love so beautiful was the freedom to choose, and he had chosen to place his love for Clara into God's hands, trusting that it would be transformed into something deeper and purer, a love that sought the good of the other without the need to possess.

The next morning, Mateo rose before the bell, slipping out of the dormitory and making his way to the chapel. He knelt before the altar, the wooden pew creaking beneath him, and bowed his head in prayer. He did not ask for the feelings to disappear, nor did he ask for the pain to be taken away. Instead, he asked for the strength to carry them, to turn them into a source of compassion rather than regret.

As the sun began to rise, filling the chapel with a soft, golden light, Mateo felt a quiet presence settle beside him. He glanced up to see Father Alvarez standing there, his hands folded in prayer, his face calm and serene in the morning glow.

After a moment, Father Alvarez turned to him, his expression knowing but gentle. "Sometimes, the hardest sacrifices are the ones we make with our hearts, Mateo," he said softly. "But remember, God sees the love you have given up, and He does not let such sacrifices go unnoticed."

Mateo nodded, swallowing the tightness in his throat. "It's strange, Father. I feel like I've lost something important, but at the same time... I feel closer to what I'm meant to do. Like I've cleared away a shadow I didn't even realize was there."

Father Alvarez smiled, a warmth in his eyes that reached deep into Mateo's heart. "That is the paradox of love and sacrifice. Sometimes, in letting go, we find ourselves more open to God's grace than we ever imagined. You are not alone in this, Mateo. Remember that."

They sat together in the chapel for a while longer, the silence between them filled with the sounds of morning—birds beginning to chirp outside, the distant murmur of the other seminarians waking for the day, and the steady, rhythmic toll of the bell calling them to prayer.

In that moment, Mateo understood that the path he had chosen would not always be easy, that the sacrifices required of him would often be painful and unromantic. But he also understood that those sacrifices were not meant to be borne in isolation. They were woven into the fabric of his life at the seminary, in the relationships he had built with his fellow seminarians, in the mentorship of Father Alvarez, and in the quiet companionship of a God who walked with him through every trial.

As the days passed, Clara continued to visit the seminary, but their conversations took on a different tone—one of mutual respect, of a friendship that was no less genuine for having boundaries. Mateo found that he could smile with her and laugh with her, even while knowing that their paths would diverge. He saw that she understood, just as he did, that some connections were not meant to be held too tightly but to be cherished for the time they were given.

And so, Mateo carried on with his studies and his prayers, his heart both lighter and heavier than before. The bell continued to ring, marking the passage of time, each toll a reminder of the commitment he had made and the love that had shaped him into something new. He knew that the temptation he had faced would not be the last, nor the most difficult. But he also knew that he was learning, slowly and imperfectly, how to navigate those temptations with grace.

One evening, as he knelt in the chapel, the memory of his final conversation with Clara drifted into his thoughts, and he found himself smiling—a smile tinged with sadness, but also with gratitude. He whispered a prayer for her, for her happiness and her journey, and then he let the memory settle into a quiet corner of his heart, where it would remain as a part of his story, a part of the man he was becoming.

When he rose from his knees and walked back into the seminary halls, he felt a sense of peace that he had not known before. It was not the peace of certainty nor the peace of a heart untroubled by desire. But it was the peace of a heart that had learned, if only a little, what it meant to let go and to trust that even in letting go, God's love could make something beautiful grow in the space that remained.

CHAPTER 14

Burdened Souls

Spring brought new life to the seminary grounds, as the once-frozen earth gave way to a carpet of wildflowers and fresh grass. The air, still cool but sweetened with the scent of budding trees, carried with it a sense of renewal. For the seminarians, the season meant preparing for Holy Week—a time of fasting, reflection, and the celebration of Christ's sacrifice and resurrection. The bells rang more often, their tones carrying across the courtyard and into the hearts of those who prayed, studied, and worked beneath their echo.

For Mateo, however, the warmth of spring and the joy of the coming Easter season did little to ease the shadows that lingered within him. The encounter with Clara had left him with a quiet ache, and though he knew he had made the right choice in letting go of the possibility of their relationship, the emptiness that remained sometimes felt like a wound that would not heal. He buried himself in his studies, seeking refuge in the teachings of the Church fathers and the rituals of the liturgy, but the silence of the chapel at night seemed to whisper his doubts back to him.

One rainy afternoon, as the sky darkened with clouds and a storm gathered over the seminary, Father Alvarez announced that they would spend the evening in the confessional—an exercise in both receiving and offering the sacrament of reconciliation. The seminarians would take turns acting as confessors to one another, practicing the delicate art of listening, of offering absolution, and of guiding souls back to the light.

Mateo felt a chill run through him at the announcement. Confession had always seemed to him a place of deep vulnerability, a space where hidden pains were brought into the open and laid bare before God. But now, the idea of standing on the other side of the confessional window—of being the one to listen, to hold the confessions of others in his hands—filled him with a sense of dread.

That evening, as the rain drummed steadily against the chapel's roof, the seminarians took their places in the wooden confessionals that lined the back wall. Father Alvarez had instructed them to offer one another the same compassion they would offer a stranger, to listen without judgment, and to remember that they, too, were in need of God's grace.

Mateo sat inside one of the confessionals, the darkness of the small booth closing in around him, He tried to steady his breath. He could hear the murmur of voices from the other booths, the low hum of whispered sins and whispered absolutions, and the rhythmic patter of the rain outside. He folded his hands tightly in his lap, feeling the rough edges of the rosary beads press into his palms, and tried to prepare his heart for what he might hear.

The curtain on the other side of the confessional rustled, and a shadow appeared behind the screen. The voice that followed was hesitant, barely more than a whisper. "Forgive me, brother, for I have sinned. It has been... some time since my last confession."

Mateo recognized the voice—it was Diego, his fellow seminarian, who had always seemed so diligent, so serious about his studies. But now, in the darkness of the confessional, there was a tremor in Diego's voice that Mateo had never heard before. He felt his heart clench with a mixture of sympathy and fear, knowing that whatever Diego had come to confess, it would not be easy to hear.

"Speak freely, Diego," Mateo said, doing his best to keep his own voice steady. "This is a place where your burdens can be lifted."

There was a pause, then Diego took a shaky breath and began to speak. "I... I've been struggling, Mateo. With doubts. With anger. I feel like I'm failing, like I don't belong here. Sometimes, I lie awake at night, wondering if God is even listening. And when I see others... people who seem so sure, so at peace with their faith, I feel ashamed. Like I'm pretending, like I'm living a lie."

Mateo listened in silence, his chest tightening with each word. Diego's confession cut closer than he had expected, reflecting struggles that felt all too familiar. He thought of his own nights spent wrestling with doubt, of the envy he had felt for those who seemed to carry their faith so effortlessly. He thought of the times he had wondered if he, too, was an imposter, someone who did not truly belong among those called to serve.

He swallowed hard, feeling the weight of Diego's pain, and realized that he did not have the words to offer easy comfort. But he also knew that perhaps comfort was not what Diego needed. Perhaps what he needed most was to know that he was not alone.

"Diego," Mateo said quietly, leaning closer to the screen, "I know what it's like to doubt. I've felt it too, more times than I can count. I've wondered if I'm worthy of this calling and if I'm fooling myself and everyone around me. But... I think part of faith is learning to carry those doubts without letting them consume us."

He hesitated, searching for the right words, and then continued. "God doesn't ask us to be perfect, Diego. He asks us to be honest, to bring our fears and our anger to Him, even when it feels like He's not listening. You're not failing because you doubt. You're still here, still seeking Him, even in the dark. And that takes more courage than you know."

There was a long silence, and Mateo wondered if he had overstepped, if his words had only deepened Diego's sense of isolation. But then he heard the sound of Diego's breath hitching, as if he were holding back tears.

"Thank you, Mateo," Diego whispered finally, his voice rough with emotion. "I... I needed to hear that. I needed to know that I'm not the only one."

Mateo closed his eyes, feeling a rush of gratitude and sorrow all at once. "None of us are alone, Diego.

That's why we're here—for each other and for God. Remember that."

He offered the words of absolution, speaking them with a reverence that he had not fully understood until now, and he heard Diego's quiet "Amen" before the shadow disappeared from the other side of the confessional. Mateo remained in the darkness, feeling the weight of Diego's confession settle into his heart alongside his own doubts.

He stayed in the confessional until it was his turn to seek reconciliation, and when he emerged, he found that his steps carried him not back to the dormitory but to the chapel's altar, where a single candle flickered beneath the crucifix. He knelt before the image of Christ, staring up at the outstretched arms and the face that bore both pain and mercy, and he allowed his own tears to fall.

"God," he whispered, his voice breaking in the quiet of the empty chapel. "I don't know if I'm strong enough for this. But I want to be. Help me find the strength to carry the burdens that are not just mine but also those of the people who trust me. Help me be a light, even when I can't see it myself."

As he knelt there, he felt the ache in his chest begin to ease, replaced by a sense of relief, as if a long-held breath had finally been released. He understood, in that moment, that Diego's confession had been a gift—a chance for him to see that he was not the only one struggling, that vulnerability was not a sign of weakness, but of a heart that was still capable of opening itself to others.

When Mateo finally rose to leave the chapel, he felt a new determination settle within him. The doubts he carried would not vanish overnight, nor would the fear that he might not be enough. But he realized that perhaps the greatest gift he could offer others—and himself—was the willingness to be present in their suffering, to carry their burdens as if they were his own.

The bell rang as he stepped outside, its familiar chime carrying through the rain-soaked air. And as he walked back to the dormitory, feeling the cool drops splash against his skin, he found himself praying not for clarity, but for the grace to walk through the uncertainty with compassion and for the strength to be a source of hope for those who, like him, were learning to find their way.

CHAPTER 15

The Shepherd's Burden

Spring deepened into early summer, and with it came new life to the seminary grounds. The cherry trees outside the chapel had shed their blossoms, leaving behind green leaves that whispered in the warm breeze. The fields that surrounded the seminary turned a vibrant shade of green, and wildflowers sprang up along the paths where the seminarians walked to their classes and evening prayers.

But even as the season brought warmth and beauty, a sense of tension lingered within the walls of the seminary. It was as if the air had grown thicker, laden with unspoken worries and hidden doubts that no amount of sunshine could dispel. Mateo felt it especially keenly, a quiet unease that gnawed at him each time he passed by the other seminarians, their faces drawn and distracted, their footsteps heavy with fatigue.

It wasn't long before he learned the cause of this tension. One evening, as the seminarians gathered in the common room to share their evening meal, Father Alvarez entered with an expression that seemed more somber than usual. He waited for the murmured conversations to quiet, then spoke in a tone that carried the weight of something he had been preparing himself to say.

"Brothers, I must share some difficult news," he began, folding his hands in front of him. "As some of you may know, the diocese is facing financial difficulties, and it has been decided that the seminary will need to make some changes. Some of our programs will be suspended, and certain positions will need to be cut."

A murmur ran through the room, and Mateo felt his stomach twist with a sudden rush of anxiety. He glanced at his friends—Emilio, Diego, and Tomás—seeing the same unease reflected in their faces. The seminary had been their home, their refuge, and the thought of it being threatened by something as mundane as money seemed almost impossible to comprehend.

Father Alvarez continued, raising a hand to quiet the growing voices. "I know this is not what any of us wanted. But I want you all to know that I will do everything in my power to ensure that your formation continues, even if it means we must adapt to new circumstances. We will be asking each of you to take on additional responsibilities to help lighten the burden for those who remain. And I ask that you continue to trust in God's plan, even when it is difficult to see."

Mateo listened, his mind reeling. He thought of the younger seminarians, many of whom had only just begun their studies, and of the teachers who had given so much of themselves to guide them. He thought of the sense of purpose he had felt when he first entered the seminary's gates and the fear that now threatened to unravel that purpose.

After the meeting, the seminarians dispersed in groups, speaking in hushed tones as they returned to their rooms. Mateo lingered in the common room, his thoughts too tangled to settle. He found himself pacing the length of the room, the words of Father Alvarez echoing in his mind.

He felt a hand on his shoulder and turned to see Tomás standing beside him, his expression thoughtful but firm. "It's going to be all right, Mateo," Tomás said, his deep voice steady. "We've faced difficult times before, and we'll face them again. This moment is just... another trial."

Mateo nodded, trying to absorb the reassurance in Tomás's words, but he couldn't shake the sense that something fundamental was shifting beneath them. "I know, Tomás, but it feels like... like everything we've been building here is in danger. What if—what if some of us are asked to leave? What if we don't have enough resources to continue our studies?"

Tomás met his gaze with a steady look, the lines of his face softened by the dim light of the common room. "Then we'll find a way to adapt. You said it yourself, back when you were struggling with your own doubts: Faith isn't about certainty. It's about walking through the darkness, even when we don't know what lies ahead."

Mateo managed a small, grateful smile. "You've been listening, huh?"

Tomás's lips quirked in a rare smile of his own. "You're not the only one who's learned a few things here, hermano."

They stood together for a moment longer, the silence between them filled with an unspoken promise—to face whatever came next with the strength they had found in each other. Mateo felt a flicker of hope stir within him, a reminder that even in the face of uncertainty, he was not walking this path alone.

The next few weeks were a blur of change and adjustment. The seminary's routines were disrupted as classes were consolidated and certain activities were suspended. The seminarians took on new duties—cleaning the chapel, maintaining the grounds, and even assisting with some of the administrative work that had previously been handled by staff members who had now been let go.

Mateo found himself spending long hours in the garden, pulling weeds and planting new rows of vegetables alongside Emilio, whose easygoing nature was tempered by a newfound seriousness. They worked in companionable silence, but Mateo could see the strain in Emilio's face, the tightness in his jaw as he pushed the shovel into the earth.

One afternoon, as they paused to rest beneath the shade of a tree, Mateo turned to Emilio, wiping the sweat from his brow. "You've been quiet lately, Emilio. What's on your mind?"

Emilio shrugged, staring down at the soil between his boots. "Just... thinking about what's going to happen. I came here because I thought it was where I was supposed to be, but now... I'm not so sure. My family's been struggling too, and I keep wondering if maybe I should go back and help them out."

Mateo felt a pang of sympathy, knowing that Emilio's struggle was one shared by many of the seminarians. "I don't know what the right answer is, Emilio. But I do know that whatever happens, you'll find a way to make a difference. Whether it's here or back in your village."

Emilion nodded, offering a small, tired smile. "Thanks, Mateo. It helps, knowing that we're all in this together."

That night, Mateo stayed up late in the chapel, the weight of his new responsibilities pressing heavily on his shoulders. He knelt before the altar, feeling the cool stone beneath his knees, and tried to find the words for a prayer that seemed too vast to contain.

"God," he whispered into the darkness, "I don't know how to lead. I don't know how to guide others when I'm still so uncertain myself. But I want to try. I want to be strong for them, to help them through this. Please... show me how."

He bowed his head, letting the silence of the chapel fill him, and in that stillness, he felt a small, quiet conviction take root. He knew that he could not change the circumstances that threatened the seminary, nor could he offer easy comfort to those who struggled with their own fears. But he could be present. He could listen. He could be a source of light, even if that light was faint and flickering.

The next morning, Mateo rose with a new sense of determination. He gathered theseminarians together after breakfast, inviting them to join him in a daily prayer circle, where they could share their concerns and support one another. The idea was met with some skepticism at first, but slowly, as the days went on, more and more of them joined.

They met in the garden, beneath the shade of the cherry trees, and took turns speaking their fears and their hopes into the open air. Mateo listened as Emilio spoke of his family, as Diego confessed his ongoing doubts, and as Tomás shared his struggle to accept the changes they were facing. And when it was his turn to speak, Mateo admitted his own fears—his worries about the future, his uncertainty about his ability to lead.

But even as he spoke, he felt the burden lighten, carried by the hands that reached out to support him. And he realized that perhaps this, too, was what it meant to be a leader—not to stand above others, but to stand with them, to be a part of the community that bore each other's burdens.

As the bell rang in the distance, calling them back to their duties, Mateo looked around at the faces of his fellow seminarians, and he saw in them a strength that went beyond their individual doubts. He knew that the challenges ahead would not be easy, that the future of the seminary remained uncertain. But he also knew that they had found something precious in their shared struggle—a faith that was not dependent on certainty but on the willingness to keep moving forward, one step at a time.

And as they bowed their heads in prayer, Mateo whispered a final plea to the God who had walked with them through every trial: "Help us to be strong, even when we are afraid. Help us to find hope in each other and to trust that Your light is with us, even when the path is dark."

CHAPTER 16

A Trial by Fire

As summer unfurled over the seminary grounds, the days grew longer and the air warmer, carrying the hum of cicadas and the sweet scent of blooming flowers. The gardens thrived under the sunlight, and the seminarians found themselves working under skies that stretched wide and blue, punctuated only by the occasional drifting cloud. The warmth brought a sense of renewal to many, a reminder that even in the midst of struggle, life continued to grow and flourish.

But the heat also brought its own challenges. The dry days grew longer, and soon the earth began to crack beneath the relentless sun. The river that wound its way through the nearby forest ran lower than usual, its waters turning from a rush to a murmur. The seminarians, working in the gardens and clearing brush from the forest paths, began to speak of the risks of drought and the possibility that the summer might prove harsher than expected.

One sweltering afternoon, as the bell rang for vespers, the seminarians gathered in the chapel for their evening prayers. The heat pressed down on them like a heavy blanket, and even the stone walls of the chapel offered little respite. Mateo knelt at his usual spot near the altar, trying to focus on the rhythm of the psalms, but his mind kept drifting to the crackling dry leaves that covered the forest floor and the way the sun seemed to bake the earth until it split open.

He had just begun to find a sense of calm when a distant shout echoed through the chapel, followed by the sound of hurried footsteps. The door to the chapel burst open, and Brother Domingo, who oversaw the maintenance of the seminary grounds, stumbled inside, his face flushed with alarm.

"There's a fire in the woods!" he called out, his voice carrying over the murmur of prayers. "We need every hand we can get—now!"

A murmur of shock rippled through the seminarians, and then they surged to their feet, their prayers forgotten as they rushed toward the door.

Mateo's heart leapt into his throat, and he felt a jolt of fear course through him. The forest was close—too close—and he knew how quickly a fire could spread in the dry summer heat.

Father Alvarez took charge immediately, organizing the seminarians into groups and handing out buckets, shovels, and wet cloths. Mateo found himself among those tasked with forming a bucket line to the river, while others ran ahead to try to dig trenches to slow the fire's advance. The air was thick with urgency, the distant crackling of the flames growing louder with each passing moment.

As Mateo joined the others in the race to the river, he felt the heat of the day intensify, sweat soaking through his shirt as he ran. When they reached the riverbank, he plunged a bucket into the water, passing it down the line as quickly as he could. The river's flow was sluggish, the water warm against his hands, but they had no time to think about its dwindling levels. Every second counted, and the fire was spreading fast.

The smoke thickened as they worked, stinging their eyes and filling their lungs with a bitter, acrid taste. Mateo's muscles ached with the effort of carrying the heavy buckets, but he forced himself to keep moving, his focus narrowing to the rhythm of the line—fill, pass, fill, pass. He caught glimpses of his fellow seminarians, their faces streaked with ash and sweat, their expressions grim but determined.

As they reached the edge of the forest, Mateo saw the flames for the first time—bright tongues of fire licking at the dry underbrush, sending sparks up into the air. The heat was almost unbearable, pressing against his skin like a living thing, and the roar of the flames drowned out everything else. He glanced toward Father Alvarez, who was coordinating their efforts with a calm authority, and felt a surge of determination. They had to stop the fire before it reached the seminary.

But even as they battled the blaze, Mateo realized that the situation was worse than he had imagined. The flames had already spread to a large patch of dry brush, and the wind was carrying embers further into the forest. They were fighting to keep the fire contained, but it felt like trying to hold back the tide with their bare hands.

At some point, in the chaos of the fight, Mateo lost track of Emilio, who had been working alongside him. He scanned the smoke-filled air, squinting against the stinging ash, and felt his heart seize when he spotted a figure moving too close to the flames. It was Emilio, struggling to pull a fallen branch away from the fire's edge.

Without thinking, Mateo broke from the line and ran toward him, his legs burning with the effort. "Emilio! Get back!" he shouted, his voice barely carrying over the roar of the flames.

Emilio looked up, his face smudged with ash, and Mateo saw the stubborn determination in his eyes. "We have to keep it from spreading, Mateo! If it gets to the thicker trees, we'll lose control!"

Mateo reached him just as a gust of wind sent a fresh wave of sparks into the air. He grabbed Emilio's arm, pulling him back, and the two of them stumbled together, falling hard onto the scorched earth. The heat was searing, and Mateo felt the edges of his clothes begin to smolder. Panic clawed at his chest, but he forced himself to focus, using the wet cloth wrapped around his hand to smother the small flames that had caught on his sleeve.

"Come on!" Mateo shouted, pulling Emilio to his feet. "We need to fall back!"

They retreated toward the bucket line, their breaths coming in ragged gasps, and Mateo felt a wave of relief when they reached the relative safety of the others. Father Alvarez spotted them and hurried over, his expression tight with worry.

"Mateo, Emilio, stay back from the fire's edge," he ordered, his voice firm. "We need you both working the line, not taking unnecessary risks. Understood?"

Mateo nodded, guilt and relief mingling in his chest. He glanced at Emilio, who looked equally chastened, and saw the fear that mirrored his own. They returned to the bucket line, focusing on the rhythm of their work, but the memory of the flames—so close, so hungry—burned in Mateo's mind.

Hours passed in a haze of heat and exhaustion, but eventually, through their combined efforts, the flames began to die down. The trenches they had dug slowed the fire's progress, and the water they carried doused the remaining embers. As the sun dipped below the horizon, leaving the sky streaked with red and orange, the roar of the blaze faded to a low crackle, and the fire's glow dimmed to smoldering coals.

When the danger had finally passed, the seminarians collapsed onto the scorched earth, their bodies aching with fatigue. Mateo sat beside Emilio, their backs resting against a blackened tree trunk, and they stared out at the charred remains of the forest they had fought so hard to save. His hands were blistered, his clothes stained with soot, but he felt a deep, overwhelming gratitude that they had managed to stop the fire from spreading further.

Father Alvarez approached, his face lined with exhaustion but softened by a weary smile. "You did well, all of you," he said, his voice rough from the smoke. "The seminary owes you a great debt."

Mateo met his gaze, feeling a swell of emotion rise in his chest. He thought of the fear he had felt, the desperation of watching the flames advance, and the realization that in those moments, he had been willing to do whatever it took to protect the place that had become his home. He had seen that same determination in Emilio, in Tomás, and in all of the seminarians who had stood beside him in the heat of the fire.

As the stars began to emerge in the darkening sky, Mateo whispered a prayer of thanks, not just for the safety of the seminary, but for the strength he had found in the midst of the trial. He understood now that leadership was not about standing apart from danger but about being willing to step into the fire with those who needed him.

And as they made their way back to the seminary, their clothes singed and their faces marked by ash, Mateo felt a new sense of resolve settle into his bones. He knew that there would be more challenges ahead—more fires to fight, both literal and spiritual. But he also knew that he would face them with the same determination, guided by the light that still burned within him and by the bonds he had forged with those who shared his journey.

Chapter 17

After the Smoke Clears

The days after the fire were filled with a strange stillness, as if the entire seminary were holding its breath. The heat of the blaze had left its mark on the forest, scorching the earth and blackening the trunks of the trees that had once stood tall and proud. The smell of smoke lingered in the air, a reminder of the struggle they had faced, and the wind carried with it a fine layer of ash that settled over the garden beds and the stone walkways like a thin, gray veil.

But within the seminary's walls, the rhythm of life continued, driven by the bell that called them to prayer, to study, and to labor. The seminarians worked to repair the damage left by the fire, clearing away fallen branches and rebuilding the sections of fence that had been charred in the heat. It was exhausting work, but there was a sense of unity in their efforts—a shared understanding that they had faced a great challenge together and come through it stronger.

Yet for Mateo, the days following the fire brought a new kind of burden. As he lay awake in his narrow bunk at night, the memory of the flames came back to him in vivid flashes—Emilio's face lit by the fire's glow, the roar of the blaze as it swept through the dry underbrush, and the moment when he had felt his own fear press against his ribs like a living thing. He remembered the desperation in his chest as he pulled Emilio back from the flames, the awareness of how close they had come to losing everything.

And beneath those memories, a deeper worry festered—one that gnawed at him with each passing day. He found himself questioning his actions, wondering if he had done enough, if he had been brave enough, strong enough. He wondered if, in his fear, he had failed to protect those who had depended on him.

It was a thought that kept him up late into the night, his mind turning over every detail of that terrible day. He began to avoid the places that had been touched by the fire, preferring the safety of the chapel and the quiet of the library. He immersed himself in scripture and theological studies, seeking comfort in the writings of saints who had endured their own trials, but the doubts lingered, like embers that refused to die out.

One afternoon, as the sun hung low in the sky and the air buzzed with the sound of cicadas, Father Alvarez found Mateo in the library, bent over a dusty volume of Thomas Aquinas. The priest's presence was so quiet that Mateo didn't notice him until he spoke, his voice gentle but firm.

"Mateo, you've been hiding yourself away," Father Alvarez said, his gaze sharp beneath his white brows. "The fire may have been put out, but I can see that something is still burning inside you."

Mateo looked up, startled by the sudden intrusion, and then sighed, rubbing a hand over his face. "I'm sorry, Father. I just... I keep thinking about what happened, about what could have happened. And I wonder if I made the right choices."

Father Alvarez nodded, pulling a chair over and sitting beside him. He folded his hands on the table, studying Mateo with a thoughtful expression. "You did what you could, Mateo. You acted with courage when the moment demanded it. Why do you question yourself now?"

Mateo hesitated, struggling to put his feelings into words. "Because I was afraid. And I feel like that fear... it held me back. When I saw Emilio so close to the flames, all I could think about was how much I wanted to save him, but also how scared I was that I wouldn't be able to."

The confession hung in the air between them, and Mateo felt a knot tighten in his throat, as if he had finally spoken something he had been holding back for too long. He waited for Father Alvarez to speak, expecting him to offer reassurance, to remind him that fear was natural, that he had done what was right.

But instead, the older priest reached out and placed a hand on Mateo's shoulder, his touch as steady as his gaze. "Fear is not a sin, Mateo," he said quietly. "It is a reminder that we are human. It is a reminder of our limits, our need for God's strength. Even Christ, in the Garden of Gethsemane, prayed for the cup to pass from him, knowing the suffering that lay ahead. But it was in a moment of fear that he found the strength to say, "Not my will, but Yours be done."

Mateo swallowed, the weight of Father Alvarez's words settling into his chest. He thought of the stories he had read, of saints who had faced trials far greater than his own, who had grappled with their own doubts and fears. He had always imagined that the faith of those saints was like a shield, making them immune to the struggles that plagued ordinary souls. But now, he wondered if their faith had been born not out of the absence of fear, but out of the willingness to face it.

"I don't feel like a saint, Father," Mateo admitted, his voice rough with emotion. "I just feel... small. Like I'm not ready for the responsibilities that come with this calling."

Father Alvarez's expression softened, and he let out a low chuckle, filled with a weary kind of understanding. "None of us ever feel ready, Mateo. But that is why we lean on God and on each other. The weight of your calling is not meant to be carried alone. It is shared—by those who came before you and by those who walk beside you."

The words resonated within Mateo, echoing through the chambers of his mind like the tolling of the bell. He thought of the moments during the fire when he had seen the determination in Emilio's face, the resolve in Tomás's steady hands, and the quiet strength in the other seminarians who had stood beside him. He realized that he had been so focused on his own fears that he had forgotten the way they had all faced the danger together, each bringing their own courage to the fight.

As Father Alvarez rose to leave, he gave Mateo's shoulder a final squeeze, his expression warm. "You have a good heart, Mateo. Trust in that and in the

God who is shaping it. And remember—courage is not the absence of fear, but the willingness to act in spite of it."

Mateo watched the priest go, the echoes of his footsteps fading into the quiet of the library. For a long moment, he remained where he was, staring down at the open book in front of him, his thoughts drifting between the pages and the memory of the flames. And then, slowly, he closed the book and stood, feeling a sense of resolution settle into his bones.

He made his way out of the library and toward the edge of the forest, where the charred remains of the fire's path still scarred the earth. He walked alone, letting the sun warm his back and the scent of pine and ash fill his lungs. When he reached the blackened edge of the woods, he paused, crouching down to run his fingers over the scorched soil.

He thought of all the things he had feared losing—the seminary, his friends, and the sense of purpose that had carried him through the darkest moments. But he also thought of what had been gained through the struggle—deeper bonds, a greater understanding of himself, and a renewed commitment to the path he had chosen.

He bowed his head, whispering a prayer for the forest, for the seminary, and for himself. And as he stood there, alone amidst the ruins, he felt a strange kind of peace wash over him—a peace that came not from the absence of struggle, but from the knowledge that he had faced it and that he would face it again if needed.

When he finally turned back toward the seminary, he felt lighter, as if a burden he had been carrying for too long had begun to lift. The bell rang out in the distance, marking the hour, and Mateo walked toward its sound, knowing that the work of healing and rebuilding was far from over.

But he also knew that he was ready for it.

CHAPTER 18

The Lost Sheep

Summer deepened, bringing with it long, hot days that stretched lazily into cooler evenings. The seminary grounds were lush and green, the gardens flourishing with the fruits of the seminarians' labor. As the days passed, the routine of life at the seminary resumed its steady rhythm, and the scars left by the fire began to heal—both on the land and within the hearts of those who had fought to save it.

For Mateo, the days were filled with a quiet sense of purpose. He continued to lead the prayer circle he had started with the other seminarians, and though the challenges they faced had not disappeared, there was a new sense of unity among them, a shared resilience that carried them through their studies and their work. Mateo felt a growing confidence in his role as a mentor to the younger seminarians, and he began to find joy in the small victories—seeing a hesitant student find their voice in prayer, or helping a struggling classmate grasp a difficult theological concept.

Yet, beneath the surface, Mateo knew that the challenges of leadership were far from over. The seminary was still struggling to adjust to the changes brought on by the financial cuts, and the weight of those adjustments was felt keenly by everyone. Tempers flared more easily, and small disagreements sometimes threatened to escalate into larger conflicts.

One evening, as the seminarians gathered for their usual dinner in the refectory, Mateo noticed a tension in the air. Conversations that had once been lively and full of laughter now seemed stilted, with more than one person staring down at their plate, lost in their own thoughts. Even Emilio, who was usually a source of lightheartedness, wore a troubled expression.

Mateo exchanged a glance with Tomás, who sat across from him, and saw the same concern reflected in his friend's eyes. Something was brewing among theseminarians—something that Mateo knew he could not afford to ignore.

After the meal, as the others began to disperse, Mateo caught sight of a figure slipping out the side door of the refectory. It was Lucas, one of the newer seminarians, a quiet young man who had arrived at the seminary just a few months before. Mateo had tried to reach out to Lucas on several occasions, but Lucas had always kept to himself, preferring solitude over the company of his peers.

Tonight, however, there was a restlessness in Lucas's movements that caught Mateo's attention. He watched as Lucas disappeared into the shadows of the garden, and a nagging sense of unease settled in Mateo's chest. He hesitated for a moment, then decided to follow, slipping out the door and into the night.

The air was cool and fragrant with the scent of night-blooming flowers. Mateo moved quietly, following the sound of footsteps through the garden's winding paths. He found Lucas sitting on a bench beneath a flowering tree, his head bowed and his shoulders hunched as if carrying a heavy burden.

Mateo approached slowly, giving Lucas time to notice him. When the younger man finally looked up, there was a flash of something raw in his eyes—something that Mateo recognized all too well. It was the look of someone who felt trapped, caught between a desire to belong and a longing to escape.

"Lucas," Mateo said softly, taking a seat beside him on the bench. "Are you all right?"

Lucas looked away, his jaw clenched tightly. For a moment, Mateo thought he might refuse to speak, but then the younger man let out a ragged breath and ran a hand through his disheveled hair.

"I don't know if I belong here, Mateo," Lucas muttered, his voice barely more than a whisper. "I thought this was what I wanted. I thought I had a calling, but...every day, it feels like I'm drifting further away. Like I'm just going through the motions."

Mateo listened, his heart aching with sympathy. He remembered his own moments of doubt, the nights when he had questioned whether he had made the right choice in coming to the seminary. He had seen those same struggles in Diego, in Emilio, and in himself.

"It's normal to feel that way sometimes," Mateo said gently. "We've all had doubts. It doesn't mean you don't belong here. It just means you're still searching."

Lucas shook his head, his expression darkening. "It's more than that, Mateo. I don't think I can keep pretending anymore. I've been thinking about leaving the seminary and going back to my old life. Maybe I'm just not cut out for this."

The words hung in the air between them, heavy with finality. Mateo felt a pang of worry, but he kept his voice steady. "Have you talked to Father Alvarez about how you're feeling?"

Lucas let out a bitter laugh, the sound harsh in the quiet of the garden. "What's the point? He'll just tell me to pray more and have faith. But I've been praying, Mateo. I've been trying to find that faith everyone talks about, and all I feel is... empty."

Mateo's chest tightened at the despair in Lucas's voice. He wanted to offer reassurance, to say that everything would be okay, but he knew that platitudes would do little to ease the ache in the younger man's heart. Instead, he reached out and placed a hand on Lucas's arm to ground him in the present moment.

"You're not alone, Lucas," Mateo said quietly, his voice filled with a quiet conviction. "I've been where you are—feeling lost, feeling like I'm not good enough. But you don't have to go through this alone. Let us help you. Let me help you."

For a moment, it seemed as if Lucas might soften, might open himself to the offer of support. But then his expression hardened, and he pulled away, standing abruptly from the bench.

"I don't need your pity, Mateo," he snapped, his voice rough with frustration. "I don't need anyone telling me what I should feel. Maybe I'm just not meant to be here."

Before Mateo could respond, Lucas turned and strode back toward the seminary building, leaving Mateo alone in the shadowed garden. Mateo watched him go, a sense of helplessness settling into his chest. He had seen the pain in Lucas's eyes, the struggle between wanting to belong and wanting to break free. But he also knew that he could not force Lucas to stay, that each person's journey of faith was their own to navigate.

That night, as Mateo lay awake in his bed, he found himself praying for Lucas—praying that the young man would find the peace he so desperately sought, whether it was within the seminary's walls or beyond them. But beneath that prayer was a deeper, unspoken fear—the fear that he had failed to reach Lucas, that he had not done enough to guide him back to the path.

The next morning, the seminarians awoke to the news that Lucas was gone. He had packed his belongings and left the seminary during the night, leaving behind only a brief note that Father Alvarez read to them in the chapel:

I'm sorry, but I can't stay. I need to find my own way.

The words were simple, but they struck Mateo like a blow. He sat in the pew, staring down at his clasped hands, feeling the weight of loss settle into his bones. Around him, he heard the murmurs of the other seminarians—some expressing shock, others disappointment, and a few whispering their relief that Lucas had made his decision before he could disrupt their community further.

But all Mateo could think about was the pain he had seen in Lucas's eyes, the unspoken plea for understanding that he had failed to answer. He wondered if he had missed something—if he had been too caught up in his own responsibilities to see the depth of Lucas's struggle.

After the service, Mateo approached Father Alvarez, who was standing at the chapel's entrance, his face lined with sadness.

"I feel like I failed him, Father," Mateo said, his voice raw with emotion. "I tried to reach out to Lucas, but I couldn't help him. Now he's gone, and I don't know if he'll find what he's looking for out there."

Father Alvarez regarded Mateo with a weary but compassionate gaze. "You did not fail, Mateo. You did what you could, and you offered him a hand when he needed it. But some journeys must be taken alone. All we can do is pray that he finds his way."

Mateo nodded slowly, but the sense of guilt remained. As he walked back through the seminary's halls, he thought about the balance between compassion and letting go—about the difficult reality that not every lost sheep could be guided back to the fold.

Yet, as the bell rang for the midday prayer, Mateo found a small seed of hope amidst the sorrow. He knew that Lucas's departure was a reminder that the path of faith was never a straight line, that each person's journey was marked by twists and turns that could not always be predicted. And he realized that perhaps the greatest act of faith was to trust that even those who wandered would find their way in time.

As he knelt in the chapel, Mateo whispered a prayer for Lucas, asking God to guide him on whatever path lay ahead. And he prayed for the strength to accept that some burdens could not be carried alone—prayed for the courage to keep reaching out, even when the outcome was uncertain.

For the first time in weeks, Mateo felt a sense of acceptance settle into his heart. He did not have all the answers, and he knew that the road before him was filled with uncertainty. But he also understood that his role was not to save everyone but to be present, to offer what he could, and to trust in a plan larger than his own understanding.

That afternoon, as he walked through the seminary gardens, Mateo came across Emilio and Tomás, who were working to repair a section of the garden fence that had been damaged by the fire. They paused when they saw him approach, and Emilio gave him a sympathetic look.

"Mateo, I heard about Lucas," Emilio said softly, leaning on the handle of his shovel. "I'm sorry, hermano. I know you were trying to help him."

Mateo managed a tight smile, grateful for the concern in his friend's voice. "Thank you, Emilio. I just wish... I wish I could have done more. I feel like I let him slip through my fingers."

Tomás set down his tools, crossing his arms as he regarded Mateo with a thoughtful expression. "You gave him what you could, Mateo. Sometimes that's all we can do. It's like the story of the prodigal son. The father let his son go, trusting that he'd find his way back in time. Maybe Lucas needs that space to figure things out for himself."

Mateo considered Tomás's words, feeling a flicker of understanding beneath the ache in his chest. He thought of the parables he had studied, the stories of wandering and return, and realized that there was a kind of freedom in letting go—an acceptance that not every journey would follow a straight line.

"I hope you're right, Tomás," Mateo said quietly, glancing up at the clear summer sky. "I hope he finds what he's looking for, wherever he goes."

They fell into a companionable silence, and Mateo felt some of the tension ease from his shoulders. Working together, they repaired the fence, hammering nails into the wooden posts and securing the loose boards. The rhythmic clinking of the hammer became a kind of meditation, a way to release the thoughts that had been swirling in Mateo's mind.

By the time the sun began to set, casting long shadows across the seminary grounds, Mateo felt lighter, as if a burden he had been carrying alone had been shared among friends. He knew that Lucas's departure would leave a mark, but he also knew that the community around him was strong enough to weather the loss, just as they had weathered the fire and every other challenge that had come their way.

As evening fell, Mateo found himself back in the chapel, kneeling before the altar. The glow of the candlelight danced on the walls, casting shadows that shifted and changed with the flicker of the flame. Mateo closed his eyes and let the silence wash over him, grounding himself in the rhythm of his breathing.

He thought of Lucas's struggles, of his own doubts, and of the countless ways their lives had intertwined for a brief moment before diverging again. And he prayed—not for a miraculous answer, but for the grace to accept that some things were beyond his control.

He prayed for Lucas's safety, wherever the younger man had gone. He prayed for the strength to continue offering support to those who remained, even when he felt unsure of his own path. And he prayed for the wisdom to see that even in the moments of loss and uncertainty, God's presence was woven through the fabric of their lives, binding them together in ways that he might never fully understand.

When he opened his eyes, the chapel was filled with the deepening twilight, the last rays of the sun streaming through the stained-glass windows. Mateo rose from his knees, feeling a new sense of peace settle into his heart, and he whispered a final word of thanks—thanks for the challenges that had shaped him and for the strength he had found in the most unexpected places.

As he stepped out of the chapel and into the warm evening air, Mateo felt the bell ring in the distance, its sound carrying across the fields like a call to something greater. He knew that the journey ahead would continue to test him, that he would face more moments of doubt and struggle. But he also knew that he was not walking alone.

And for the first time in a long while, that knowledge felt like enough.

CHAPTER 19

The Fracture

The days grew hotter as summer stretched on, and the air inside the seminary became heavy and oppressive, like a blanket that refused to be lifted. The cool mornings quickly gave way to sweltering afternoons, where the sun baked the stone walls of the chapel and the gardens wilted under its relentless heat. Even the bell, so constant in its rhythm, seemed to toll with a weariness that matched the mood of those who lived within the seminary's walls.

For the seminarians, the season brought with it a restlessness that was hard to ignore. The challenges of recent months—the uncertainty brought on by the financial cuts, the trauma of the fire, and the unexpected departure of Lucas—had left their mark.

Though most of them tried to carry on with their studies and duties, there was an undercurrent of tension that simmered just beneath the surface, like embers that could catch fire at any moment.

Mateo noticed it in the small things—snappish words exchanged over chores, the way some seminarians seemed to avoid one another's eyes during meals, and the uneasy silence that sometimes settled over their prayer sessions. He tried to address it in the way he knew best, gathering the others for moments of shared reflection, offering a listening ear when someone needed to talk. But he could feel the strain building, and he feared that it would only take a small spark to set everything ablaze.

That spark came on an afternoon when the heat was at its worst. The seminarians had gathered in the garden for a work session, tasked with clearing a section of overgrown brush that had taken root along the seminary's perimeter. Sweat soaked through their robes as they hacked at the stubborn weeds, their movements sluggish in the stifling air.

Mateo was working alongside Emilio and Tomás when he heard raised voices nearby. He turned to see Diego and another seminarian, Carlos, standing a few paces away, their faces flushed with anger. Diego's hands were clenched into fists, and Carlos's expression was one of frustration, his gestures sharp and agitated.

"You think you're better than the rest of us, don't you, Diego?" Carlos spat, his voice loud enough to draw the attention of the others. "You are always lecturing us about how to do things the 'right' way. Maybe you should worry more about yourself than about the rest of us!"

Diego's face darkened, and he took a step closer, his posture tense. "I'm trying to hold us to a higher standard, Carlos. We're here to serve God, not to coast through our duties like they don't matter. If you can't handle that, maybe you're the one who doesn't belong here."

Mateo felt his stomach twist as the words echoed through the garden. He dropped his gardening tool and moved quickly toward them, hoping to defuse the situation before it escalated further. Around him, the other seminarians had stopped working, their expressions a mix of curiosity and unease.

"Enough, both of you," Mateo said firmly, stepping between Diego and Carlos. He placed a hand on each of their shoulders, trying to project a sense of calm despite the tension crackling in the air. "This isn't the place for this kind of argument. Let's take a breath and talk it out later, all right?"

But Carlos shook off Mateo's hand, his eyes blazing with frustration. "Talk it out? That's easy for you to say, Mateo. You've always been the one everyone looks up to, the one who's got everything figured out. Maybe you don't know what it's like to feel like you're not good enough, like you don't measure up."

The words stung, and Mateo felt his own temper flare, a rush of heat rising to his face. He opened his mouth to respond but then caught himself, taking a deep breath and forcing himself to stay composed. He could see the hurt beneath Carlos's anger, the way it mirrored some of the same doubts he had seen in Lucas before he left.

"Carlos, I don't have everything figured out," Mateo said quietly, his voice steady but filled with an edge of emotion. "I'm struggling too. We all are. But turning on each other isn't going to make it any easier."

Diego's expression softened slightly, but Carlos's anger seemed only to harden. He crossed his arms over his chest, glaring at Mateo as if daring him to challenge his words. "Maybe some of us don't need your help, Mateo. Maybe we're tired of being treated like we can't stand on our own two feet."

Mateo felt the weight of the words settle heavily in his chest, but he knew that arguing would only deepen the rift that had already begun to form. He stepped back, trying to find a way to bring the tension down.

"Let's take a break," he said, raising his voice so that the other seminarians could hear. "It's too hot to keep working like this. Go cool off and get some water. We'll finish up later."

There was a moment of hesitation, but then the seminarians began to disperse, muttering under their breath as they made their way back toward the seminary building. Diego shot Carlos a final glare before turning to follow them, his shoulders hunched with tension. Mateo watched them go, feeling a deep sense of weariness settle over him.

Tomás approached, his expression troubled. "That could have gone worse," he said, but there was a note of doubt in his voice. "I don't know what's gotten into everyone lately. It's like we're all on edge."

Mateo nodded, running a hand through his damp hair. "It's the pressure. Everything we've been through... it's wearing us down. And I don't know how to make it better."

Tomás placed a hand on Mateo's shoulder, giving him a reassuring squeeze. "You're doing your best, Mateo. We all see that. But maybe it's time to let Father Alvarez know what's going on. He might have some wisdom to offer."

Mateo hesitated, then nodded slowly. "You're right. I'll talk to him."

That evening, Mateo found Father Alvarez in his study, surrounded by books and papers. The older priest looked up with a welcoming smile when Mateo knocked on the door, but his expression turned serious when he saw the tension in Mateo's face.

"Mateo, come in. What's on your mind?" Father Alvarez asked, gesturing for him to sit.

Mateo took a deep breath, then explained what had happened in the garden, recounting the argument between Diego and Carlos and the sense of division that seemed to be growing among the seminarians. As he spoke, he felt a knot of frustration and sadness tighten in his chest, a feeling he had been trying to keep at bay.

"I've been trying to keep everyone together, Father," Mateo said, his voice thick with emotion. "But it feels like I'm failing. I don't know how to reach them anymore. It's like... everything is coming apart."

Father Alvarez listened intently, then leaned back in his chair, his gaze thoughtful. "It's not easy to lead when those around you are struggling, Mateo. But sometimes, the best thing we can do is acknowledge the pain that's already there. Pretending that everything is fine only deepens the wounds."

Mateo nodded, absorbing the words, but his thoughts were still tangled. "What do you think I should do?"

Father Alvarez offered a gentle smile, the lines around his eyes deepening with age and wisdom. "Gather the seminarians tomorrow. Let them speak openly about what they're feeling—about their fears, their frustrations, and even their anger. It might be messy, but it will be honest. And honesty, Mateo, is the first step toward healing."

The next day, Mateo did as Father Alvarez suggested. He called the seminarians together in the chapel, where light streamed through the stained-glass windows in muted colors. The air was still thick with heat, but the stone walls of the chapel provided a small measure of relief. The seminarians took their seats in the pews, their expressions wary but curious.

Mateo stood at the front of the chapel, feeling the weight of their gazes on him. He took a deep breath, then spoke from the heart.

"I want you to know that things have been difficult lately," he began, his voice steady but carrying the raw edge of his own emotions. "We've all been through a lot—the fire, the changes in the seminary, even losing friends like Lucas. I know that many of you are struggling, and I know that it's easy to take that pain out on each other. But we don't have to face it alone. We can face it together."

He paused, letting the words sink in, and then he gestured for the others to speak. Slowly, haltingly, the seminarians began to open up—about their worries for the future, their feelings of isolation, and their frustrations with the changes in their routine. Diego spoke of the pressure he felt to live up to his own expectations, while Carlos admitted that he often felt like he was falling short compared to others.

As the confessions spilled into the open air, Mateo felt a sense of relief wash over him. The tension that had built up over the past weeks began to unravel, replaced by a sense of understanding that had been absent for too long. They did not solve all their problems in that one meeting, but they had taken a step toward something better—toward a community that could face its struggles honestly, without turning against itself.

Afterward, as the seminarians dispersed, there was a tangible sense of release in the air, like a tension that had finally found its outlet. Mateo remained in the chapel, watching as the others left in small groups, their expressions lighter than before, their voices softer. He saw Diego and Carlos exchange a brief, awkward nod—a small gesture, but one that carried the promise of reconciliation.

Tomás approached Mateo, a weary but genuine smile on his face. "That was a good idea, hermano," he said, clapping Mateo on the back. "We needed that. You did well."

Mateo smiled, though he felt a lingering ache in his chest. "I'm not sure if I did enough, but I think... I think it's a start."

Tomás nodded, his expression thoughtful. "It's more than a start, Mateo. It's a reminder that even when things seem to be falling apart, there's still a way to come together. You helped us see that."

They stood in silence for a moment, taking in the quiet of the chapel and the way the evening light streamed through the stained-glass windows, casting a kaleidoscope of colors across the stone floor. Mateo felt a sense of gratitude welling up inside him—not just for the small victories of the day, but for the friendships that had carried him through the darkest moments.

As the last of the seminarians left the chapel, Father Alvarez appeared in the doorway, watching them with a quiet smile. He nodded toward Mateo, a gesture of approval that filled him with a warmth he hadn't realized he needed.

"Thank you, Mateo," Father Alvarez said as he joined them. "You gave the others a chance to be heard, to share their burdens. That is no small thing."

Mateo looked down, feeling a little embarrassed by the praise, but he managed a small smile. "It wasn't just me, Father. They were the ones who were brave enough to speak."

Father Alvarez's smile deepened, the lines around his eyes crinkling with warmth. "Perhaps. But sometimes, it takes one voice to open the way for others. You were that voice today."

Mateo accepted the words with a quiet nod, but he knew that the challenges they faced were far from over. The doubts and fears that had surfaced during the meeting would not disappear overnight, and the tensions that had simmered for so long could not be healed with a single conversation. But he also knew that they had taken a step forward, that they had begun to mend the fractures that had threatened to divide them.

As the evening turned to night, Mateo lingered in the chapel, kneeling before the altar with a heart that felt both lighter and heavier than before. He thought of Lucas, of the struggles that had led him to leave, and he hoped that wherever he was, he had found a measure of peace.

And he thought of the other seminarians—Diego, Carlos, Tomás, and Emilio—each of them carrying their own burdens, their own doubts and dreams. He prayed for them, for the strength to face whatever trials lay ahead, and for the grace to continue growing together, even when the path was difficult.

The bell rang, its sound carrying through the stillness of the night, and Mateo rose to his feet. He walked back through the seminary's halls, feeling the cool night air brush against his skin, and he allowed himself to hope that tomorrow would bring a new beginning.

CHAPTER 20

A Crisis of Brotherhood

As summer reached its peak, the heat grew more oppressive, pressing down on the seminary like a heavy hand. The air shimmered with warmth, and the seminarians found themselves seeking shade whenever possible, resting beneath the branches of trees or in the cool shadows of the chapel's stone walls. The garden thrived despite the heat, but every task felt like an ordeal under the unrelenting sun.

Amidst the sweltering days, a new tension began to settle over the seminary—one that was less obvious than the earlier disagreements but more insidious, creeping into their conversations and routines like a slow-moving shadow. The long days and mounting pressures seemed to take their toll on the friendships that had once felt so steady, and Mateo sensed the shift with a growing unease.

It began with small things. Emilio, usually so cheerful and talkative, became quieter, his jokes less frequent. Tomás seemed to carry a deeper weight in his shoulders, his normally confident stride growing slower and more burdened. Diego, who had once been quick to offer insights during their study sessions, now spent more time alone, sitting in the garden with a distant look in his eyes.

Mateo tried to reach out to them individually, inviting them to share their thoughts, but each conversation seemed to stall before it truly began. Emilio would shrug and brush off his questions with a forced smile, while Tomás would mutter that he was "just tired" before changing the subject. Diego, when pressed, would only offer a vague assurance that he was "working through some things" on his own.

For the first time, Mateo found himself feeling isolated among his friends, as if they were all drifting away on separate currents. He continued to lead the prayer circle and continued to offer what support he could, but he couldn't shake the feeling that something crucial was slipping through his fingers—something he wasn't sure how to hold onto.

One evening, as the sun dipped low on the horizon and the cicadas droned in the trees, Mateo decided to take a walk through the seminary grounds, hoping that the movement might help clear his mind. The air was still thick with heat, but there was a faint breeze stirring the leaves, offering a small respite. He wandered down a familiar path that led through the garden and toward the river, where the water ran shallow and clear.

As he neared the riverbank, Mateo caught sight of Emilio sitting on a fallen log, his head bowed and his shoulders slumped. He paused, wondering whether he should leave Emilio to his thoughts, but something about the way his friends sat—so still, so uncharacteristically subdued—compelled him to approach.

"Emilio," Mateo called softly, stepping closer. "Mind if I join you?"

Emilio glanced up, and for a moment, his usual smile flickered to life, but it quickly faded. He gestured for Mateo to sit, his gaze turning back to the water. "Sure, Mateo. It's a free country, isn't it?"

Mateo lowered himself onto the log beside Emilio, letting the coolness of the river air brush against his skin. For a while, they sat in silence, the sound of the flowing water filling the space between them.

Mateo took a deep breath and then decided to speak honestly.

"I've noticed that you've been... quieter lately," Mateo said carefully. "I'm worried about you, Emilio. We all are."

Emilio let out a low, bitter laugh, the sound rougher than Mateo had ever heard from him. "Yeah, well, maybe you're not the only one going through stuff, Mateo. We've all got our demons, you know?"

The words were sharp, almost cutting, and Mateo felt a pang of hurt, but he forced himself to stay calm. "I know you're struggling, Emilio. I just wish you'd let us help. Whatever's going on, you don't have to go through it alone."

Emilio's hands tightened into fists on his knees, and he stared down at the ground, his jaw clenched. For a long moment, Mateo thought he might refuse to speak, but then the tension seemed to break, and Emilio let out a shaky breath.

"It's my family, Mateo," Emilio said quietly, his voice barely more than a whisper. "My father's business back home is failing, and they don't have enough to make ends meet. They keep telling me not to worry about it, that I should focus on my studies, but... how can I? I feel like I should be there, helping them, not sitting here in this place where I'm not even sure I belong."

Mateo felt his heart ache at the rawness of Emilio's confession. He reached out, placing a hand on his friend's arm. "I had no idea, Emilio. I'm so sorry. I know how much your family means to you."

Emilio shrugged, his expression crumpling into a look of despair that he had clearly been trying to hide. "I've been thinking about leaving the seminary, Mateo. I want to go back home and try to do something to help my family. But every time I think about it, I feel like I'm failing—like I'm walking away from something I thought was my calling."

Mateo's chest tightened with empathy. He thought of Lucas, of the struggle between duty and desire, between the path he had chosen and the pull of those he loved. "You're not failing, Emilio," he said firmly. "Wanting to help your family doesn't mean you're turning your back on your calling. It means you care. It means you have a heart."

Emilio looked at him, and for the first time, Mateo saw the depth of pain in his friend's eyes—pain that had been hidden behind so many easy smiles. "But what if I'm not strong enough, Mateo? What if I'm not strong enough to stay here or to leave?"

Mateo squeezed his shoulder, trying to convey all the reassurance he could muster. "You don't have to decide this alone, Emilio. We're here for you—Diego, Tomás, me, and even Father Alvarez. Whatever you decide, we'll support you. But you have to be honest with yourself about what you need."

For a moment, Emilio said nothing, and Mateo wondered if his words had made any difference. But then, slowly, Emilio nodded, a tremor running through him as if he were releasing a breath he'd been holding for too long.

"Thank you, Mateo," he said, his voice rough with emotion. "I'll... I'll think about it. I promise."

They sat together by the river until the light faded, speaking little but sharing the comfort of each other's presence. Mateo felt a small measure of hope bloom within him—hope that Emilio, at least, was beginning to open up, to let some of the weight he carried be shared.

But a sense of unease lingered, a shadow that followed him back to the seminary and into the days that followed. He spoke with Tomás and Diego about what Emilio had shared, and together they tried to find ways to support their friend—to give him space when he needed it and to stand by him when he struggled. Yet even as they worked to lift each other up, Mateo knew that the tension in their group was only a reflection of the larger uncertainty that haunted the seminary as a whole.

In their private conversations, Father Alvarez offered Mateo words of encouragement, reminding him that the road to priesthood was never a straight path and that each of them would face moments of doubt and crisis. But even as he listened, Mateo could not shake the fear that they were on the edge of something fragile—something that might break if pushed too far.

One evening, as a thunderstorm rolled in over the hills, bringing with it the promise of rain, Mateo stood by the window of his dormitory, watching the sky darken with heavy clouds. He thought of all that had happened since he had arrived at the seminary—of the friendships he had built, the challenges he had faced, and the moments of grace that had come in the unlikeliest places.

He thought of the fire, of Lucas's departure, of Emilio's quiet pain. And he realized that beneath it all, he had come to care for each of them in a way that he had never expected—had come to see them not just as fellow seminarians but as brothers on a shared journey.

And perhaps, Mateo thought, as the first drops of rain began to fall against the windowpane, that was what it meant to be called to this life—to care deeply, to feel the weight of each other's struggles, and to continue walking forward together, even when the path was uncertain.

As the rain poured down, washing the heat and dust from the air, Mateo whispered a prayer for his friends, for himself, and for the strength to face whatever trials lay ahead. He knew that the coming days would bring new challenges—challenges that might test the bonds they had built. But he also knew that they would meet those challenges together, with hearts that were open and hands that were willing to reach out.

And in that moment, as the storm raged outside and the bell rang softly in the distance, Mateo felt a sense of peace settle over him—a peace born not from certainty, but from the quiet, unyielding hope that they would find their way through the darkness, side by side.

Epilogue

Through his conversation with Emilio, Mateo confronts the difficult balance between individual desires and communal responsibilities. He recognizes the burden that each of his friends carries, realizing that sometimes the greatest act of leadership is not guiding others but simply being present with them in their pain. Yet, even as he manages to offer some comfort to Emilio, the tension that looms over the seminary community feels like a storm cloud that refuses to clear.

The next day, the rain from the night before had left the air cool and fresh, the garden beds glistening with droplets that clung to the leaves and flowers. Mateo hoped that the downpour might have washed away some of the heaviness that had settled over them, but as the seminarians gathered for breakfast, the atmosphere remained subdued. He exchanged a glance with Tomás, who gave him a small, encouraging nod, as if to remind Mateo that they were in this together.

But the sense of unease only grew stronger as the week went on. Despite their efforts to support each other, the reality of the seminary's challenges loomed large, casting a shadow over their daily routines. The constant pressure to balance their studies with their additional responsibilities began to wear on them, and even the smallest disagreements seemed to carry the weight of larger frustrations.

It was during one such moment, as they gathered in the common room for a brief break between study sessions, that the tension finally boiled over. Diego, who had been unusually quiet throughout the morning, suddenly slammed his book shut, the sound echoing through the room like a gunshot.

"I can't do this anymore," Diego snapped, his voice thick with frustration. "All this talk about faith and calling, but what good is any of it when everything around us is falling apart? We're supposed to be preparing for a life of service, but I can't even focus on my studies with all these distractions. It's like the seminary doesn't care if we succeed or fail."

Mateo felt the air leave his lungs, the shock of Diego's outburst hitting him like a blow. Around the room, the other seminarians exchanged uneasy glances, but no one spoke. Mateo looked at Diego, seeing the pain and exhaustion etched into his features, and he realized that his voice was more than just frustration—this was the voice of someone who felt like he was losing hope.

"Diego, I know it's hard," Mateo said gently, trying to keep his emotions in check. "But we have to hold on. We have to believe that what we're doing here matters, even when it's difficult to see."

Diego's eyes flashed with anger, and he rose to his feet, pacing the length of the common room like a caged animal. "That's easy for you to say, Mateo. You're the one everyone looks up to, the one who always seems to have the right words. But what about the rest of us? What about those of us who aren't sure we even belong here anymore?"

The accusation stung, and Mateo felt his composure slip. He rose from his seat, facing Diego directly, his own frustration bubbling to the surface. "You think I don't struggle too? You think I don't have doubts? I've questioned my place here more times than I can count. But I'm still here, Diego. I'm still trying, because I believe that we're meant to do this together."

For a moment, Diego's anger faltered, a flicker of uncertainty passing across his face. But then he shook his head, his expression hardening. "Maybe you're right, Mateo. Maybe you do belong here. But I don't know if I do."

With that, Diego turned on his heel and stormed out of the room, leaving a stunned silence in his wake. Mateo stood frozen, the weight of the confrontation pressing down on his chest. He felt Tomás's hand on his shoulder, offering a wordless gesture of support, but it did little to ease the ache that had settled into his heart.

"I'm worried about him, Mateo," Tomás said quietly, his gaze fixed on the door through which Diego had just disappeared. "He's been struggling for a while, but this... I've never seen him like this before."

Mateo nodded, swallowing against the tightness in his throat. "I know, Tomás. I'm worried too. But I don't know how to reach him anymore."

They spent the rest of the day in a state of uneasy anticipation, wondering if Diego would return and if he would be willing to talk. But as the hours passed and the evening bell rang, marking the time for vespers, Diego remained absent. Mateo's concern deepened, a knot of anxiety twisting tighter with each passing moment.

After the evening prayers, Mateo found himself standing outside the seminary gates, staring out into the fading light of the summer dusk. He thought of the conversations he had shared with Diego over the months, the moments of laughter and camaraderie, and the quieter times when they had spoken of their shared hopes and fears. He realized that he couldn't bear the thought of Diego walking away from everything they had built together—walking away, perhaps, with the same sense of despair that had driven Lucas to leave.

Just as Mateo was about to turn back toward the seminary, he caught sight of a figure moving through the twilight, approaching the gates with slow, uncertain steps. It was Diego, his shoulders hunched and his face shadowed by the dimming light. Mateo's breath caught in his chest, and he hurried forward, meeting Diego just outside the gates.

"Diego," Mateo said, relief flooding his voice. "I'm glad you came back. I was worried."

Diego let out a weary sigh, rubbing a hand over his face. "I'm sorry for what I said earlier, Mateo. I didn't mean to take it out on you. I just... I feel like I'm drowning, and I don't know how to make it stop."

Mateo felt a surge of empathy, and he reached out, gripping Diego's arm with a firmness that he hoped conveyed his sincerity. "You're not alone, Diego. We're all struggling, but we're struggling together. Let us help you. Let me help you."

Diego looked up, meeting Mateo's gaze, and for a moment, his expression crumpled, revealing a depth of vulnerability that he had kept hidden for far too long. "I don't know if I can keep going, Mateo. I don't know if I'm strong enough."

Mateo's grip tightened, and he spoke with a conviction that came from the deepest part of his heart. "You are strong enough, Diego. You've already proven that just by being here and facing it every day, even when it hurts. And if you feel like you're drowning, then lean on us. Lean on me. That's what we're here for."

For a long moment, Diego said nothing, his expression wavering between doubt and hope. Then, slowly, he nodded, his shoulders sagging as if he were finally allowing himself to let go of some of the weight he had been carrying.

"Okay," Diego whispered, his voice barely audible. "Okay, Mateo. I'll try."

They walked back to the seminary together, side by side, the cool night air brushing against their faces. Mateo felt a sense of relief wash over him, but he also knew that this was only the beginning of a longer journey—one that would require patience, understanding, and a willingness to face the darkness together.

As they reached the seminary gates, the bell rang out in the distance, its sound clear and unwavering, cutting through the stillness of the night. Mateo paused, glancing up at the tower where the bell swung, a small but constant presence that had marked every turning point in his life here.

And he realized that, like the bell, they would continue to ring out, to call each other back from the edge of despair, to remind each other that they were not alone. It would not be easy—there would be more moments of doubt, more nights when the way forward seemed uncertain—but they would face those moments as they always had: with open hearts, with hands ready to reach out, with a faith that was not in having all the answers but in walking the path together.

As Diego turned to him with a tentative, grateful smile, Mateo returned it with one of his own, feeling a small ember of hope reignite in his chest. And he whispered a silent prayer of thanks—for the bonds that had carried them this far, for the strength they had found in each other, and for the courage to continue on, regardless of what trials the future might hold.

(Continued in "When The Music Gets Louder")